The Man Who Rode His 10-Speed Bicycle To The Moon

To Barbara and Owen

The Man Who Rode His 10-Speed Bicycle To The Moon

Bernard Fischman
Illustrated by Barbara Lanza

Richard Marek Publishers
New York

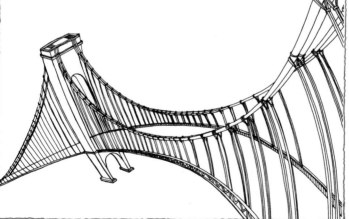

Library of Congress Cataloging in Publication Data

Fischman, Bernard.
   The man who rode his ten-speed bicycle to the moon.

   I. Title.
PZ4.F5283Man   [PS3556.I765]   813'.5'4   78-23730
ISBN 0-399-90038-1

The Man Who Rode
His 10-Speed Bicycle
To The Moon

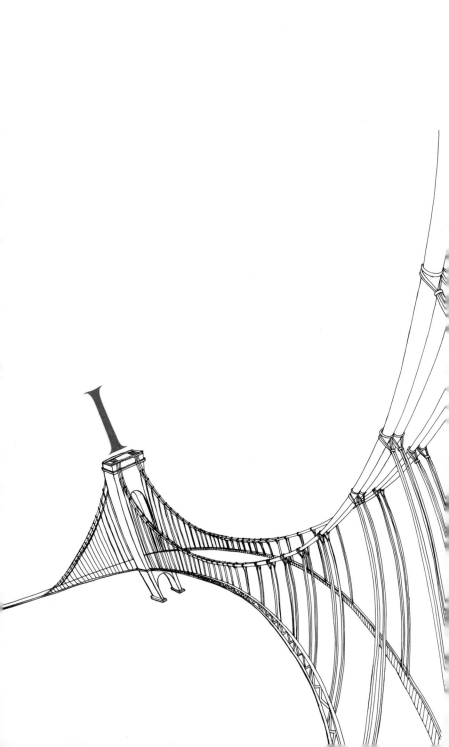

Stephan Aaron was not certain he existed. Frequently he felt he was becoming transparent, paradoxical for a man over six feet tall with bushy, black beard and dark, shell-rimmed glasses that made even his smallest expression appear unyieldingly intense. Yet, more and more, Stephan found himself experiencing the odd sensation that people could pass right through him. And did.

He considered his problem with a certain amusement and detachment that always infuriated those closest to him, particularly Dorothy, his wife. He did not discuss it; his dialogue was completely internal. Yet, certain facts seemed to contradict his strange new feeling. The beautiful Dorothy; his success as one of New York's top graphic designers; his dog, Sam, the huge, white Great Pyrenees, who daily padded alongside him on walks to Riverside Park. And then there were those acquisitions which included a big, Upper West Side apartment, a house in Connecticut, annual trips to Europe, an Italianate-Red Alfa Romeo in his garage.

One unchanging fact, however, kept cropping up: Stephan Aaron felt nothing. Anger, love, sadness, contentment. Nothing. To exist is to feel, and to *know* you feel. Try as he might, Stephan felt nothing. And if nothingness is analogous to transparency, then Stephan Aaron was fast disappearing off the face of the Earth.

But why? How? When did it start? Although he only sensed changes stirring inside, certain benchmarks stood out: the past summer, for instance, the summer he was to be forty-five. To anticipate that event, Dorothy had given him a ten-speed bike.

For some time, Stephan had wanted—or, at least, thought he wanted—a ten-speed bike. It was the New York thing to do. It was exactly right for a man soon to be forty-five. Or so it seemed.

One of Stephan's first experiences with transparency began as he and Dorothy watched the ringlet-haired young man who was assembling his new bike. The boy was efficient, so consumed in creating a sonata of flying wheels, chain, crank, gears, the proper saddle height. Even Dorothy seemed hypnotized by the process, a process that bespoke a world of action, excitement. A world that made Stephan feel like an outsider, shut out.

"Come on," the boy had said to Stephan and Dorothy, "I'll try it for you."

He sprang into the saddle, pirouetted, spun, dashed, and stopped the bicycle in hard skids until Stephan was certain the slender frame would snap.

"Got to make sure it works," he said. "Now, you try it."

He handed the bike to Stephan. Dorothy smiled.

"Reassuring me," Stephan thought. He knew it was already too late.

The position was wrong. He had to lie parallel to the cross bar, arc his head back. That made his neck ache. What about the brakes? Not controlled by the pedals, but by levers on the handlebars! And he must not only remember, but find the shifts!

Upper Broadway is no place to

learn to ride a ten-speed. Double-parked cars forced him to swerve into the middle of the street. He had to fight hostile taxis and drivers anxious to make the lights. A blue-nosed whale of a bus nearly crushed him against a row of parked automobiles. He was certain the driver saw him and had deliberately tried to kill him. Slowly.

His legs cramped, his back ached. This was not anything he had hoped it would be. He was a ridiculous, frightened, middle-aged man in bicycle shorts.

The silky, wet-eyed girl who screeched to her friend, "*Mira! Mira!*" did not help. Even Dorothy, who watched with pride and concern, made him feel embarrassed. He got off, promising the boy, Dorothy, and himself that he would try again somewhere in less traffic. Dorothy and the boy both assured him that that was the thing to do.

But after a few more essays along Riverside Drive and another on Broadway, the ten-speed was parked in the foyer of their apartment. Where it stayed.

His defeats on the bicycle symbolized his withdrawal, this immutable retreat into transparency. At another time he would have attacked the bicycle with manic ferocity. Not now. Why?

He could see no tangible reason. His studio and his reputation were only getting bigger.

His marriage was familiar, defined; Dorothy managed their lives with asperity and efficiency. Everything was under control. Such tight control.

Except, perhaps, Sam, who was, like Stephan, growing older. Sam still moved with dignity; the huge square head erect, the soft gray eyes quietly taking in everything. But Stephan noticed an occasional drag to Sam's hindquarters. That was just a little stiffness, nothing more? No? Could it be that Sam was dying?

He could not bear to think it. For Stephan was like many of us who are afraid to admit they love, hate, are afraid or, worst of all, *feel* their feelings.

He knew Dorothy sensed his malaise, but he was not certain whether she regarded him with pity or disinterest. They were going in different directions; now it was becoming more apparent to both. Yet, they tried.

They took the bike to the farm. That did not work either. Country drivers push old pickups gouged with rust over roads at brutal speeds. Stephan was no match for suicidal Neanderthals. Again, the ten-speed came to rest in the hallway, another artifact to be someday restored, along with the rest of the country house. Perhaps.

By the end of summer, Stephan knew he needed time and space. He wanted to talk to Dorothy, but he did not know what to say. Instead, he first made an arrangement with his partner, Sherman, to take work to the country, to keep in touch, and to visit the city periodically. Sherman grudgingly agreed with a cryptic, "Do what you have to do."

When Stephan stepped out of their office, a lovely old brownstone diagonally across from the Museum of Modern Art, the September haze suspended the city in the same kind of limbo Stephan felt himself. Yet he also perceived the glimmerings of a new freedom. The meeting had been easy, the difficulty would be explaining to Dorothy.

Explain? What? He did not know himself. That evening when he told her, he again felt his transparency, as if he watched someone else lecture Dorothy on some sort of philosophical dilemma. He realized

5

that such standing aside protected him from the hurt he was causing them both. His only solace was the knowledge Dorothy's own perceptiveness surely had made her aware of their schism. She seemed to agree to accept his decision, but not quite certain why. She even helped him pack, going through the motions as if in a dream.

At last the time came to go. He got the leash for Sam, who waited patiently in the hallway, knowing the signs of packing meant he was going to the country. Dorothy held the door for him. As he pushed the button for the elevator, they both looked at each other. Stephan had a strange sense of *déjà vu*. It was almost as if the same excitement with which they had regarded each other on their first meetings was rising again, only now they were both looking in different directions.

"I wish," Stephan said, "there was a villain in this piece."

Each knew there was none. Except, perhaps, time.

"Goodbye," she said. "Keep in touch."

"I'll keep in touch," he answered. "Take care of yourself."

Then the elevator doors closed and they dropped out of each other's lives.

He drove to the house in Connecticut and then began a period in Stephan Aaron's life when time was out of joint.

He took long rides in the country; watched the autumn come down on the hazy Litchfield hills. When the sun was warm, he walked out in the back field with the old dog, who grew noticeably weaker and weaker.

6

He could not think of Sam dying. Occasionally, the dog, feeling his old self again, would lie on the ground and move his paws to make angel-wing patterns in the dirt. But it was obvious his life was ending.

And as Stephan watched Sam fade, he saw his own life diminish, too. Little interested him or had value. On his trips to New York he did not see Dorothy. He knew she must be angry, hurt, as she had a right to be.

Then a strange thing happened to Stephan. On one of his visits to the city he met Pia.

He was not quite sure how it happened. He had left the office one evening just at twilight and decided to sit in the garden of the Museum of Modern Art. The great glass windows of the museum shimmered ebony. Birds moved in the trees or fluttered to the walks for crumbs. Outside, the city moved in easy symphony. Inside, only the sound of the fountains.

Stephan was seated watching the fountains when he became aware of someone speaking to him. He turned and saw, in the chair next to him, a lovely young woman holding a book. When he had sat down, no one was on either side of him. Although he may have been daydreaming, he felt sure he would have noticed her. But there she was, speaking again.

"I said," she repeated, "you are one of the most beautiful men I have ever seen."

He did not know how to answer. Even seated she appeared tall, slim, with light chestnut hair tied up around her head. She wore a loose-fitting blouse, seersucker skirt. Her legs were smooth and brown. She looked directly at him. Not staring, looking.

He felt inept, uneasy. Not only because of her directness, but that he could not explain her presence. Was she merely being friendly? Should he say something? Did the heavying twilight reduce tensions, enable people to communicate more easily?

"This is the first time anyone has ever told me I was beautiful," he said at last.

"Well, you are. Somebody should have told you long ago."

Something seemed to tell Stephan she knew a lot about him. Certainly there was a knowing. Was it that hint of a smile, the open expression in her eyes that made her seem so omniscient? Intriguing, but it also made him uneasy, perhaps even a little frightened.

Stephan wanted to continue the conversation, but did now know how. She seemed content to let talk lag. The next move obviously was up to Stephan. But what?

As he debated, the guards busied themselves, making semi-surreptitious moves, the straightening of chairs, quick tracks through the crowd to remind everyone that the garden *did* close.

"Goddamn it!" the girl suddenly exploded. "I wish they wouldn't do that!"

"Do what?" Stephan asked, knowing what she was referring to.

"Going through that stupid closing-time ritual. It's, it's totally unnecessary. Doesn't that make you angry?"

Again Stephan was embarrassed. He was trying to appear relaxed, but the girl mirrored his own feelings exactly.

"Why don't they just say, 'piss off,' or 'get out'? I

could deal with that," she went on. "Oh, no, they would never dare."

"Well, you certainly say what you think, and right out. Do you do that all the time?" Stephan asked. He was relieved he had found some corridor into her being.

"I don't know. I just do it," she answered.

Now she was irritated with him. Perhaps she had expected him to say something to the guards, or at least be more honest with what he was feeling. She was right. He was detaching himself and he hated himself for it.

"You really connect up with what you feel right away, don't you?" he asked. "How do you do it?"

"I'm a witch."

"A what?"

"Yes, a witch."

In the softening twilight and the mysterious way she seemed to have appeared, Stephan was almost ready to accept that somewhat startling admission.

"Does that frighten you?" she asked. She was smiling. "You don't know whether to believe me or not, do you?"

"No."

"Then don't."

"But tell me," Stephan said, "are witches, or whatever you are, always so direct in saying what they feel?"

"I don't know. I only say things like that to people who I think will understand."

"And you think I understand?"

"Really," she said, almost patronizingly, "you must stop that, you know. You're still doing it."

"Doing what?"

"Pretending something is not happening, trying to be cool. But you know that, don't you?"

She saw right into him. He felt vulnerable, yet excited that she was obviously interested in him.

"Look," he said, trying to show some initiative. "I've never met a witch before. Would you like to have a cup of coffee with me? Or do witches have coffee?"

"Oh, they do! They do!" she said. "And it would be marvelous, but not tonight. I have to meet some friends. Say, would you like to come along?"

"Are they witches, too?"

"No, of course not, just really nice people. Why don't you come?"

Stephan wanted to, but held back.

"No," he said. "I have to drive to Connecticut, so, actually, I think it's better I get started."

"Oh, where?"

He told her, and described the big, old colonial. He knew he was trying to impress her.

"Gee," she said, "that sounds fabulous. I'd love to see it."

"Great, when can I show you?"

"Soon," she said. "Look, I really must run. Here take this, this is my address." Quickly she took a page from a small, blue, lined notebook, wrote her first name, "Pia," and her phone number.

"Why don't you call me? I really would like to see you. You must forgive me for running, but I'm late. Damn it, I'm always late! Will you call?"

"Yes, of course."

She took his hand briefly, smiled, rose and left. As

he watched her mount the steps, Stephan knew summer was over, and he still could not explain how she had appeared.

Winter came down hard and windy on Connecticut. The farmhouse grew colder. Outside it was damp and raw. Each morning he looked at Sam and the dog looked back, both of them knew what was coming, Stephan unable to accept. Was it possible this was the dog who only a few short years ago had run with such powerful strides after bicycles in Riverside Park, who had reared up five feet on his back legs and with deep, baritone growls in his throat, wrestled with Stephan? Was this the dog kittens used to sleep upon, on whom children used to ride in the lobby of their apartment building?

Sam looked at Stephan as the only one who could help. Immobile, almost completely paralyzed, all he could do was lie in the feeble sunlight. As the night fell, he would struggle to his feet and put his great head in Stephan's lap. Stephan would stroke the silky ears, but he could not look into Sam's eyes.

Finally, as winter's pain became unbearable Stephan accepted what he had to do. He owed this great friend the dignity of a clean, final end. He phoned the vet, arranged to have Sam put down. Damping his feeling so he was only going through motions, he bundled the dog into the car. They were waiting for him. He took the big dog out and half carried him gently to the door, where the vet's assistant waited. She came down the stairs in her white coat and took Sam, whom she had known for years. She led him up the stairs, his ears flat against his head as they always were when he knew he was going into something he did not like.

"I can take it from here," she said. "Will you be back, later?"

"No," Stephan said. "You take care of the rest. I won't be back."

He stroked Sam's head, and then the Great Pyrenees was gone, through the door. The last Stephan saw of him was his magnificent tail, still carried in a proud plume above his back.

As Sam disappeared through the door, Stephan fought the hysteria that made him want to go after the old guy, bring him back. But he could not. Sam was on his way, Stephan on his.

In later days Stephan could not remember how he got the car started, how he continued down the road. He knew the only thing for him to do was not to think, not to think anything at all. He did not know how he could stay at the farm.

Fortunately for Stephan, two of his dearest friends, both teachers, were off to London for a year. They had told Stephan many times before that their Manhattan apartment near Gramercy Park was his to use whenever he wished and had left their keys for him with a neighbor. He had thought about coming back. Now was the time.

That very day he packed his clothing and drove to New York. As soon as he could, he phoned Dorothy and told her what he had done. Her first question was, "Are you all right?"

He was grateful for her asking. It was one of the few times in their life that she had reached out to him so spontaneously. "Yes," he said, "I'm all right now,"

12

and then he had to hang up, not certain he was telling the truth. Or if anything would be right again. What remained was to wait winter out, reading, getting used to the apartment, allowing the hard edge of cold to soften into a new season.

That early spring he lived as if suspended. Evenings, he wandered along Third Avenue, the mildness of the season consonant with his mood. Flower stores stood bunches of fresh-cut daisies on the sidewalks and laced their windows with lilies of the valley. On First Avenue fruit stores were filled with explosions of color, light-green beans, darker avocados, yellow grapefruit and bananas, a mélange that shimmered and lit the air with soft pungencies. Among it all, Stephan walked, withdrawn, but content, content to heal with spring.

He called Pia, and she was delighted to hear from him. They spent a Sunday afternoon drinking coffee, talking. She did not refer to herself as a witch, nor did he. Instead, she was just a beautiful woman. So beautiful Stephan had difficulty believing she really wanted to be with him. For some reason he felt he had to point out that he was over forty. She chided him and he did not pursue it. Neither made a motion toward anything more; conversation was enough. Besides, Stephan was afraid of love.

For some weeks an occasional meeting with Pia and the walks sufficed. It was enough, this sleepwalking, but gradually Stephan realized he wanted something more.

When he returned to the city, Stephan had brought the ten-speed with him. Why, he was not sure. He knew that he was going to ride it. But when? Then, one evening, quite precipitously, he decided to ride.

It was the time of the spring easiest to be in, night comes on so unceremoniously, twilight seems forever.

Stephan felt himself brave enough to bike into the Village. He discovered the New Port Alba Restaurant on Thompson Street, where he had a marvelous meal. Afterward, the light was still strong enough to ride the few blocks into Soho. His bravado amazed him. Normally he would have returned to his apartment. But tonight another force seemed to invite him on. And as he rode, something strange began to happen.

He seemed hardly to pedal. The bike glided down West Broadway, across Spring Street and Canal almost on its own.

Shifting was so simple! He realized what the young man had been trying to explain. All you must know is to *anticipate* a hill; move to the proper gear *before* the rise; the energy output remains the same, smooth and easy. He began to feel at one with the machine as he slid farther and farther south, past Watts Street and Desbrosses Street, past Laight, Hubert, Beach and North Moore, names he never knew existed before, lined with silent warehouses.

Although the steel doors were rolled shut, and quiet draped the platforms, the twilight combined with elixirs that vibrated around darkening buildings lavendered by the setting sun. He turned west on North Moore to Hudson, pedaling through still heaving perfumes of jasmine and spice, basil, thyme, lemon and tea.

On he went, now down Greenwich Street, past rows of canopied buildings that seemed to echo in muted music the mazurka of traffic that flowed during the day. Most were dirty; none lost any dignity.

"How wonderful!" he thought. "It's as if I'm standing still and the entire Earth turns under me."

And, as he continued, he became less and less aware of any energy the bicycle demanded of him. He moved with no effort at all.

He rolled past the warehouses and moved toward lower Wall Street. The towers of the World Trade Center caught a final silvering coda of light. The black facades surrounding the promenades, cavernous, cool. No people.

He floated down Church Street haloed in color. At last, he reached the dark mass of Battery Park, tipped with lamps along the walks. He moved past the squat, circular building that had once been the Aquarium. He remembered again, as a boy, the feeling of being immersed in the luminous tanks where gray shadows of sharks coasted and turned. They never should have moved the Aquarium, he thought.

A few people still walked along the water's edge, but most were other cyclists who wheeled and spun, just like he, with no visible motion or energy to propel them. At the end of the promenade, a television crew.

"What are you covering?" Stephan asked as he rode up.

"Oh," one answered, "some ex-GIs are trying to take over the Statue of Liberty. We're just waiting to see what will happen."

Stephan, put off by this intrusion, quickly turned around and began to pedal back into the softening darkness. He seemed to blend with a rhythm that was part of the buildings, that held him in a kind of luminescence that pulsed above the moving cars.

As he rode back from the World Trade Center, Stephan had the strange sensation he was floating, that the wheels did not actually touch the ground. What else could account for the ease with which he traveled? It hardly seemed possible he had traveled well over five miles from the Village, down to the Battery and back on his first big ride. He could look down at the wheels and see if he flew, but he preferred not to know.

Instead, he thought, how nice it would be if everyone could fly. If only now and then. To be free—to be detached from the friction of reality—or, at least, those realities that finally wear us down to tears.

When was the last time he had cried? He remembered the burning in the eyes, the tight throat, the sensation of being too full, too full. Was it the quiet, the joy of the ride, the sense of himself that made him feel like crying now? He was elated; his eyes brimmed.

"How beautiful," he thought, "to be able to cry."

A new warmth and sense of self flooded him. He delighted immersing himself in the interplay of headlights and shadows that fell in the canyoned streets. Once, in glimpsing down a cross street, he thought he even spotted a rider on an old-fashioned two-wheeler, a "penny-farthing" with the huge front wheel, tiny one in back. How deliciously right for this old-fashioned bicycle to be in the oldest part of New York. He wished he could find the cyclist, congratulate him. Yet he wondered if the rider might have felt out of place.

"Nonsense," he thought. "I'm the one who feels out of place."

But he had a momentary vision of himself on the old bike trying to explain himself to crowds who watched. Then he rode on.

He was not at all tired when he got back to his

apartment, and he was beginning to be aware of a strange sensation, an innate knowing, that on a bicycle such as his a man could go anywhere.

Anywhere.

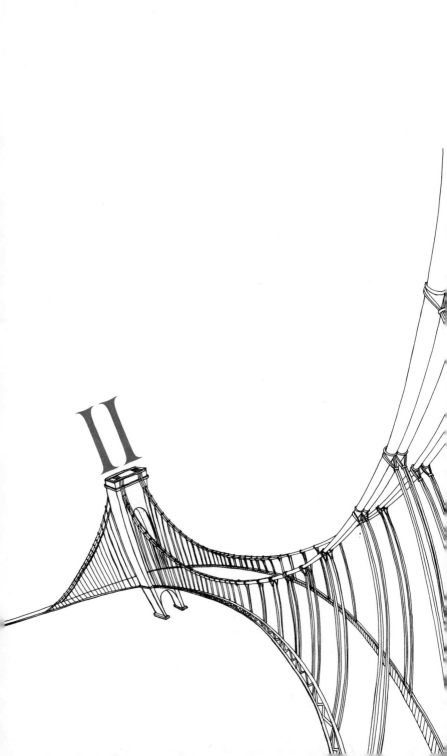

In the weeks that followed, insights deepened into confidence. Discovery no longer merely amazed. A simple mathematical equation existed between the gear ratios. One could make a ten-speed bike function exactly in terms of one's personality. Low gears for hill climbing, relaxing, looking about. A quick shift to the higher sprockets when one felt racy and daring.

Nevertheless, he still felt a certain triumph in the easy way he made the bicycle obey. He became bolder. If he could go as far as the World Trade Center and back, why not more?

And so, one clear, spring Sunday morning he began the classic venture: Central Park. From his apartment he pedaled leisurely toward Irving Place.

He sensed a truce between himself and the automobiles. The drivers resented him, but put up with him. The rules were simple: Be creatively assertive, but always play it safe.

Across Third Avenue he leveled out to the quiet of Irving Place, then rode around Gramercy Park. The high iron fence on one side, the heavy stone buildings around the perimeter, made him feel as if he were riding through a medieval town.

At Madison Square Park the sun came down in unyielding brilliance. In the cool of the morning a few persons already lounged on benches reading. He pedaled up Madison Avenue, quieter than ever before, practically no traffic.

But there he learned the first brutal law of bicycling. He had gone by the Morgan Library, carefully keeping to the left, away from the merciless buses. He bumped joyfully across Forty-Second Street, past Brooks Brothers, French-Shriner and the other men's clothing stores who advertise every Sunday in the *Times.* He had become wily enough to anticipate cars on crosstown streets, what he did not account for was traffic coming from behind.

Suddenly, a car with Jersey plates caught up with him, then slewed around him and, making a left turn, cut him off. No horn, no warning, just a screech of tires and a black metal torpedo that cornered into him. He wrenched the handlebars and spun the bike, one foot skidding on the street. The car ticked his rear wheel and threw him against the curb. He was not hurt, but he was frightened, angry.

Now he knew it was not enough to watch for crossing traffic. Drivers can and will sneak up behind cyclists and suddenly turn across their path. Right of way means nothing. Certain drivers hate bicyclists. Lesson number one.

New York on Sunday is special. Freneticism leaves. Buildings stand pure and cool, islands of glass with displays in darkened ground floor windows. Traffic lights change in long rows of red or green. Even the people seem not to be in a great hurry. Many of them carried the *Times* or the Sunday *News,* with its multicolored boxes of the comics laced under their arms. A few tourists pressed noses into open maps, hesitated at corners.

At Sixty-First Street he headed toward Central Park. He crossed Fifth Avenue at the Plaza, fringed with ice cream trucks, balloon vendors, a man with dancing dolls on an invisible string, and huge bouquets of people that fanned out into the park. No automobiles!

He started north up the drive, the short strip of grass between him and the walk to the children's zoo. Frisbee players swept yellow and blue arcs against the early green of the trees. He pedaled up the hill. Horse manure smelled fresh and sweet. He rode for a few moments beside one of the carriages and listened to the silk-hatted driver give his tour lecture. The passengers smiled at him and he smiled back. They seemed a little self-conscious, as if they knew the park really belonged to him.

At the top of the drive he merged with other cyclists. Now the bicycle seemed to take wings as he rolled down the slight hill where the road divides to Seventy-Second Street. Cyclists had strewn on the grass themselves and their bikes, and were divided almost evenly into *Times* readers or sunbathers. He pedaled on, feeling superior when he thought he spotted people on rented bikes.

He dipped down past the boat rental docks, then up to the top of the hill. He had to work, but at least he did not worm left and right as did some of the others. At the top, the Metropolitan Museum of Art, then the long level stretch that parallels upper Fifth Avenue.

The sunlight cut down between the trees and once again he had the sensation he was flying. The bicycle required absolutely no effort. He looked down at the front wheel. No, it rolled merrily along on the ground. He twisted around to look at the back wheel, and nearly lost his balance. The bike veered crazily across lanes. Other cyclists shouted. One blasted his police whistle in short, angry bursts.

Stephan pulled over to the side to regain his composure. He pretended to check the back wheel.

"Chain slip?" asked a young man who was talking to a pretty girl. Their bicycles rested against a bench. Obviously they had seen Stephan and this made him even more self-conscious. The girl looked at him and smiled; the last thing he wanted was sympathy.

"No, I don't think so," he answered. "Everything seems all right."

"Maybe you hit some wet leaves." The roadway was perfectly dry, but Stephan appreciated that.

"Maybe I did."

"You have to watch out, some of those riders go pretty fast."

"Yes," said the girl, "they act as if they're on speed trials."

True, many bicyclists in Central Park seemed to treat the roads as if they were a private racing preserve. Stephan was somewhat overcome by the efforts of both these two nice young people to put him at his ease.

"Okay," the young man said, "take it easy, watch the leaves!" They all laughed and with that remounted their bikes and rode away easily, powerfully. Two of those amiable, terribly efficient children of the sixties.

Stephan watched them pedal away. He was certain they would have understood the real reason he nearly fell.

Now he was more relaxed. Just before he had tried to look at the wheels he had been feeling so good, so free. He was aware of people around him, but he seemed to be in other space. Where, he could not say. As the bike skimmed along he had felt he was on the verge of discovering something, something he had been very close to on that very first ride. For the moment, he had lost it. Not totally, it was there, and he was going to reach it. Somehow the bike connected it all; how, he could not guess. But he knew he was going to find out, soon.

He remounted and doubled back to Seventy-Second, where he came upon the carnival that begins at the Bethesda Fountain and flows down the Literary Walk.

The band shell sparkled with a group of mimes. He watched them, enchanted. Graceful, precise, intense, they moved with a kind of poetry that communicated something inside, something the onlookers felt and responded to. He wished he could be up there with them, if only in the background, letting others know he was there, but not really having to commit himself.

Balloons floated above the green benches where lovers and old people sat, some watched the performance, some talked. Riders with helmets and gloves and caps, turned up in the mode of professional cyclists, wheeled amongst the Frisbee players. Stephan found he, too, was perfectly able to maneuver around strollers. He learned how to back-pedal to keep his balance, to toe-push where the crowd got too dense.

He stopped to listen to a group of folk singers, was taken particularly by a man who sang very professionally, but whose dark eyes stared straight ahead with a sense of madness. Stephan bought a hot dog. He sat on one of the benches and watched. The sound of folk singers, tape recorders, and voices blended magically with the aroma of charcoaling beef, hot dogs, and popcorn into a haze of laughter and smoke.

He was hot, tired, and content. The crowd moved in a swirl of muted noise and color. He spread his arms along the back of the bench and leaned his head back. He felt he was slipping into some kind of delightful trance, buoyed up by the sound and movement all around him.

Then it happened.

He heard, or rather sensed, something moving. He tried to lift his head but could not. He felt sleepy, almost paralyzed. His head wanted to loll back. He had difficulty keeping his eyes open. Whatever it was drew nearer. Stephan felt he should get up to look, but he could not. His eyes teared from the sun; his vision swam.

And then it appeared: the giant, old-fashioned two-wheeler he had seen or imagined he had seen following him in the Battery. The rider towered above the crowd, bobbing heads a sea that bore him along. Strangely, no one seemed astonished. Yet the rider, whoever he was, was so strangely out of place. For some reason, Stephan felt both a sense of embarrassment and pity for the rider so obviously trying for attention—in all the wrong ways. Again, Stephan could imagine himself on that old-fashioned two-wheeler. He wished the rider would go away. He did not belong, a feeling Stephan knew only too well.

As the anachronistic cyclist drew closer, Stephan tried desperately to see his face, but the sun prevented Stephan from focusing. All he could see was a figure dressed in knickers and broad, striped stockings, a blue, long-sleeved shirt.

Despite the fact he could not see the rider's face, Stephan recognized something familiar. The body, its

25

movements, the way the hands held the handlebars all reminded Stephan of someone. But who? Worse, Stephan sensed the rider was looking for him.

As the bicycle drew closer, Stephan's embarrassment grew. He would not know what to say or do. What was the rider looking for? What did he want? Stephan clenched his eyes tightly closed, as if that would shut the rider out.

Stephan was paralyzed, he was certain the rider knew he was there. He tightened up, waiting, but for what? Sounds blended into a continuous roar. He heard voices, but could not identify words. He knew there was laughter, perhaps at both of them? He waited, his entire body clenched until it seemed he could stand it no longer. Then he sat up, moved his arms from behind the back of the bench, and looked around.

The crowds continued to surge by. No sign of the antique bicycle. Or its rider. Although just as many people walked on the promenade, the atmosphere was quieter, more relaxed. Stephan looked up and down. Still no sign.

Had the rider, hurt, simply ridden away? Would it have been so much for Stephan to have acknowledged him? To nod, to recognize, to help?

He did not feel he had been asleep, yet he knew he had not imagined it all. Not twice. Someone *had* ridden by, just as there *had* been someone riding near the Battery.

As casually as he could, he asked a man sitting next to him, "Did you see him?"

At first, the man did not reply. Stephan asked again.

"See him? Who? What? You see all kinds here, mister." And, as if to confirm his own convictions, the man got up and moved away before Stephan could say another word.

Strangely, when he began to ride again, he felt ashamed, yet relieved. The experience on the bench far behind him, he had been successful in staying in his own little world. Success?

"Never have I been so alone," he thought. The sight of the spectral bicyclist had somehow sharpened the feeling.

Toward the end of the afternoon, as the spring sunshine laved him with gold, he rode out of the park, through the Grand Army of the Republic Plaza, past the Plaza Hotel, Bergdorf Goodman, and into Fifth Avenue. Again, a sense of joy seemed to permeate him and the crowd, but left him strangely detached. The buses wallowed and roared along the right, traffic flowed speedily down the center, but did not interfere with him. Masses of people moved on the sidewalks.

It was at Fifth Avenue and Forty-Second Street he learned the second lesson that was going to be the most important of all.

Coming up Fifth Avenue, against the traffic, was a young black boy on a stripped-down bicycle. He wore tight blue shorts, white tank top, white tennis shoes, and socks halfway up his thin calves. The bicycle seat was extremely high, the frame huge. He looked like a giant bird.

North-south traffic had stopped. East-west traffic roared across Fifth. Bothered not at all, he turned into the crossflow. He had made his decision; regardless of the light or the traffic, nothing was going to stop him.

27

Horns shrieked, cars slammed on brakes, people turned to stare. At one hideous moment, an automobile spurted across Forty-Second Street one way, a cab another, the boy locked in their path. Stephan was certain he would be killed, but the boy leaned back, pulled up on the handlebars and the bicycle leapt off the ground. The front wheel reared, the bicycle pirouetted between the two vehicles, hurdling a small space. The cars jolted to a halt. But to the boy this ballet was a daily act of life. And, as the bike arced down, he lifted one hand, not in a gesture of defiance, but a cavalier, exuberant wave, a salute to the crowd and to himself.

"That bicycle," Stephan thought, "actually left the ground. If he wanted, he could have kept on going, straight up to the sky!"

The lights changed and Stephan moved forward with the rest of the traffic. The boy far out of sight.

Now Stephan knew what he had only sensed before. As he pedaled down lower Fifth Avenue, quiet and still in the late afternoon sun, his loneliness left him and he smiled to himself. He possessed a secret. He was yet to understand it all. Yet he knew he would. Now he was content to enjoy the beginning: He did not look down, but he knew his wheels did not touch the ground.

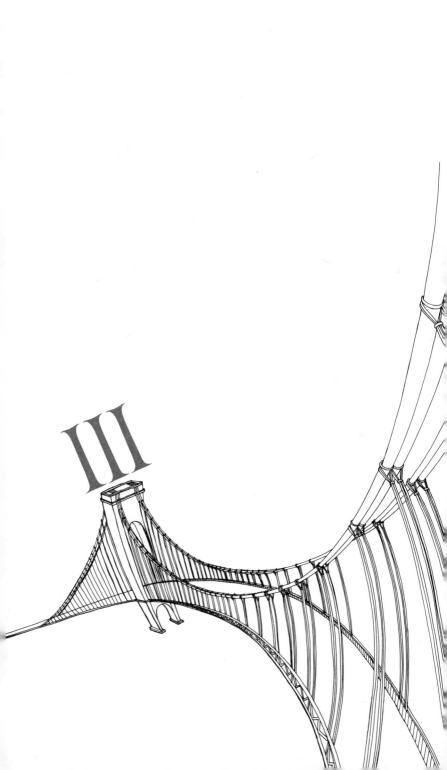

III

"To fly," Stephan thought a few nights later as the summer evening deepened and street sounds arabesqued around the apartment windows like flights of hummingbirds.

To fly, to feel the surge of the bicycle as it lifted up and away. No strain, no breathlessness, instead, a force within him that moved him gently but purposefully ahead.

Sitting in the armchair, he became drowsy and let himself float away.

Now, once again on his bike, he skimmed along, the merest fraction of an inch above the ground. A marvelous secret. And how wonderful! He could go anywhere, not just Central Park, or the Battery, but along highways, lanes, and hidden roads. He went into the hills of Connecticut, past old colonials, gleaming white, and massive maples that fire autumn red and yellow. The sudden unexpected glimpse of a lake shining in the sun where the road dipped to its shore.

Now he was working in the garden. From nowhere, voices floated toward him the same way the hum of a bee gradually impinges on consciousness. They told him there was more than one person, not the neighbors, no one in an automobile. The voices were hushed, but happy. He stood up, noting the cramp in his back from bending so long, and saw a group of eight or ten cyclists. Only their heads and shoulders were visible, the bicycles still hidden by the rise of the road. They all seemed to float.

Bright red and blue pennants swayed above their heads. They pedaled leisurely, talking an almost secret language, one filled with joy. Little exclamations flitted up, bits of laughter dappled the air. The men wore striped shirts, the girls, lightly colored blouses. It was almost as if a bouquet of flowers passed along the road. No sound from the tires, muted on the soft asphalt. As if they were suspended, so silently did they move.

They saw him, smiled and beckoned.

Suddenly, he was beside them on his own bicycle, pedaling happily.

They went everywhere, no place too far, too difficult to reach. Over the highways of New England, across midwestern plains, down long reaches of roadway that stretch to the deserts of the Orogrande Mountains.

Sunlight lit the ridges of Sleeping Elephant Mountain, the clear desert air opened up space so they could see almost to Mexico. Red sand banked against iron rocks glowed with inner heat, a sudden rainstorm whipped out of the mountains, pearling the cactus with droplets. Later, the sage, wet with the cold rain, glowed amethyst, radiating the final light of the sudden, violent sunset.

Distance became intense, stretching out and expanding upon itself until it seemed great billows of light would carry them into infinity.

On, on, across the desert, over the Rockies and down their windward side to the Pacific, north on 101 to Big Sur, the Canadian Rockies, the arc to Alaska, the Aleutians, and down the coast of Japan, Thailand, Indochina, India. Their wheels sang over the highways, dirt roads, freeways. Across jungles, deserts, great rivers and oceans. Brown legs and arms moving rhythmically as they pedaled the world. Wherever they went, they were enveloped in a silent, mystical joy. Always above them, the flashing pennants.

He must tell Dorothy!

He stood in front of their apartment building and waited for her. Then she came out of the lobby wheeling the most beautiful ten-speed, chrome bicycle he had ever seen. It was so beautiful, he forgot about his singing, magical voyage. They were going to ride together!

She stood, waiting for his approval.

He could only nod, but then they both smiled, accepting each other. Together, they raced down to the promenade on the lower level of Riverside Park.

The park was strangely quiet, different.

As they rode, he felt great tenderness toward her. And he thought she leaned toward him, wanting to feel him against her, too. No one else was on the walk, and he wondered how it would be to take her in his arms. It was going to happen, soon, but he could hardly believe it. All the tension was gone and they laughed, looking at each other with secret knowing as they pedaled on and on, faster and faster.

For some reason, they stopped. Dorothy got off her bike and watched Stephan. He was going to teach her how to shift gears, but he felt he was showing off.

She appeared tense, but interested.

He tried desperately to make it look easy. He made large ovals so he could get up better speeds, announced what he was about to do and tried to time his shifts to the exact point when he drew abreast of her.

32

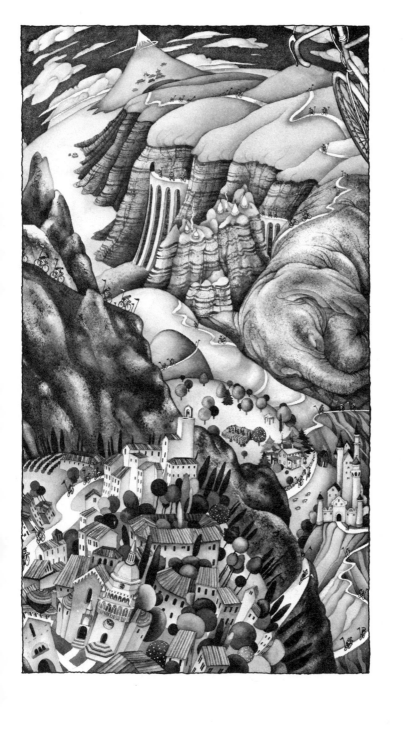

He felt she wanted to try it herself, but he could not stop himself.

He rode in larger circles, shifting down, shifting up. He brought the bike to nearly a standstill and then began a slow, upward crawl through the gears. Then he repeated this procedure, each time a little faster, his turns more complex. He saw that Dorothy was getting uneasy, felt he should stop, let her try.

But he was so immersed in his own pyrotechnics that he did not notice he had turned off the main walk, was out of sight on a bypath.

At the peak of his triumph he looked for her, but she was gone! All at once, the bicycle seemed heavy, harder to pedal. Impossible that he had done something wrong. Darkness was coming. He tried to race along the walk, pedaling faster, but the bicycle got heavier.

Then he saw her, a small figure walking alone. Her bicycle leaned against one of the benches, unattended. He got off his own bike and ran along, calling, "Dorothy! Dorothy!"

At first she did not seem to hear him; then she stopped and waited. He felt foolish. He dismounted, pushed his own bike to the bench, collected hers, and wheeled both toward her.

Dorothy, to his surprise, did not appear angry. She was calm, very much in control. In fact, she smiled a slight smile which frightened Stephan.

As he came closer he could think of nothing to say.

"Do you want to try it again?" he finally asked.

She shook her head. No.

"But why? I thought you wanted to."

She did not answer. Instead she began to move away.

34

He stood, paralyzed.

"Why are you leaving me?" he cried. He was in tears, hysterical. Sobs came up in great gasps. Tears burned in his eyes.

Dorothy still moved away.

"Why are you leaving me?" he repeated. "Please! Don't leave me!"

She turned and gave him a compassionate smile.

"Please!" he cried once more.

She stood there gently smiling. For a moment things seemed to be all right. Then she began to disappear.

He opened his eyes. Closed them. Again there was the sense of her. Then the feeling of her presence was gone.

Stephan sat up in his chair.

His chin had been pushed down against his chest, a wet slice of perspiration under his neck. His back was cramped and he had been clenching his hands so hard his arms ached.

He stood up in the darkened room and went to the window. Outside, on First Avenue, the lights had come up and the neon in the stores across the street glowed green and red. Down on the street, two boys performed on skateboards, whirling in dizzying circles. Around them, carefully keeping out of their orbit, another boy pedaled on his hi-rise bike. Tree branches partially hid them from Stephan, but he knew they were there.

No matter how daring their turns and attacks, they were constrained to the street, and always would be.

He was tired; his throat was dry. Glimpses of the dream came back to him. He still felt that terrible desperation as Dorothy moved away. He knew now, as he had sensed so painfully in the dream, she was gone.

He felt empty, alone.

"That is the way it is," he thought. "The way it really is. I never flew. I will never fly."

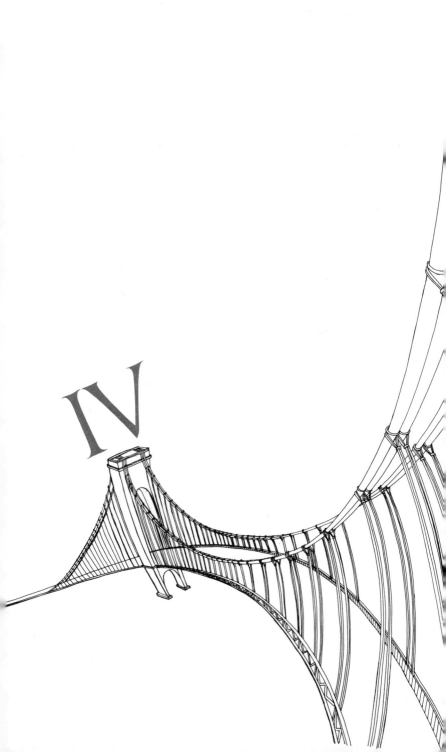

IV

During the time he bicycled—
exploring an old world that was for him a new
world—he forgot his loneliness, how he missed
the white Great Pyrenees. When he rode, he was in
another dimension, he seemed another person, the
mime he had pretended to be on the stage. The dis-
coveries he made all seemed to come from someone
else, someone drenched in sound and color. But
when he put the ten-speed back in the apartment, he
remembered. Not just that the big white dog was
gone, and Dorothy, but that his whole life lacked col-
or. He was numb, the apartment numb, the world
numb. At work he functioned efficiently, as if in a
dream. He felt content only when he rode.

Even when he walked on the streets it was not the
same. Summer flowed around him. The trees caught
the lights from street lamps haloed by mists of moths.
Heavy buses heaved up Third Avenue. Shop windows glowed. He tried not to see all the young people
in love. But he did.

Was it to be this way forever? Was he to go to his
office every day, smile politely in the halls, do his
work, eat by himself, come home evenings to the
apartment alone? Where was the hero who rode the
bicycle?

And who was that hero? Not unlike that almost pa-
thetic rider of that old-fashioned two-wheeler, so obviously seeking attention, noticed by no one. Was he,
Stephan, the same? Was he transparent still? Even
when he was on the bike, moving with the crowds in
the park, feeling warm and responsive to them, no
one saw him. No one smiled at him. Did he smile at

them? He thought so, felt so. But was it all inside? How was it possible that no one responded to all his good feelings? Why did no one speak? Why did pretty girls pass him on the streets? Did anyone see him?

He was riding on the transverse at Seventy-Second Street, absorbed in these gloomy questions and surrounded by an assortment of Sunday morning cyclists, when suddenly Pia appeared. She materialized at his side so abruptly that he almost believed her declaration to be true: She *was* a witch. One capable of popping up in his life at just the right time.

She stopped her bike expertly. Stephan stopped, too, and, exuberantly, she gave a short burst of applause.

She was wearing very short, white shorts, a blue and white, striped T-shirt. Her long chestnut hair flowed behind her, almost down to her waist. No transparency. She was real and vibrantly alive.

"I think you *are* a witch," Stephan said. "I didn't see you at all."

"Of course I am. Didn't I say so?"

"You did, you did."

"Get me something cold to drink, I'm thirsty."

"Champagne?"

"Orange soda."

"Done, and done," he said, and they walked their bikes to a bench and Stephan bought two cans of orange soda. When he sat down, she moved close to him. He liked that very much.

"Is this what witches do on their day off?" he asked.

"Oh, come on. Stop teasing me, and teasing your-self."

"Myself?"

"Of course. As long as you keep calling me a witch, you don't have to treat me like a woman."

"But, you were the one . . ." he started to say and then laughed.

She didn't answer although he knew she was aware of what he meant.

They sat quietly. The cheap orange drink tasted good.

"Best champagne I've ever had," he said.

"Me, too."

"You know," he said after they both had remained still for a while. "I've just made a great discovery."

"What's that?" she asked. This time she sounded more serious, less effervescent.

"Young people . . ."

"Young people!" she interrupted. "Stop trying to put distances between us. You always make refer-ences to your age. Do you think you're so old?"

"Yes, I'm beginning to."

"Well, you're not, and I wish you would stop bring-ing it up all the time."

"Do I?"

"Yes."

"I'm sorry. I guess ·you're not going to let me finish."

"Oh, I am! I am." Once again her gay self. "I love to hear you talk." And she put her forehead against his shoulder and gently shook her head.

He wanted to reach down and stroke her hair, but before he could, she straightened up and looked at him expectantly.

40

"Well?" she asked.

"Now I'm afraid to say it."

"Why?" she asked.

"Because now it sounds like I'm making too much of it," he answered.

"Well," she said, "why don't you just go ahead and say it?"

"Okay," Stephan answered. "It's simply this: Young people are just as smart as old people."

"Young people are just as smart as old people?" she said incredulously. "Did you think that 'old people'— whatever that may mean in that protective vocabulary of yours—have some God-given right to be smarter than young people?"

"Yes," he said, "as a matter of fact, I think I did. I think that's a built-in given that we use as a club."

"Well," she said, "there's no question about that. But tell me—when did you make the great discovery that we're just as smart as you?"

"Just now," Stephan answered.

"Just now?"

"Yes," he said. "I suppose I've realized it for some time, but this is the first time I've been willing to admit it in public."

"Well," she said. "Would you like me to call a few more young people to sit around at your feet?"

"No," he said. "I'm going to allow you to carry the message forth."

"That I will, that I will," she said. "But tell me, now that you've made this great admission, what is your advantage?"

"My advantage?" Stephan asked.

"Yes. Now that everybody is equal, what gives old people the edge?"

41

"Experience," Stephan answered.

"Experience? I bet I've had more experiences than you," she said.

"Yes, I'm sure you have," Stephan answered, and held his hand up in surrender. "Suppose we just ride. Would you like to ride the ten-speed?"

"I was hoping you would ask," she said. "I've ridden them before, but I can't get used to the gears."

He explained them patiently. At first she could not find the ratios that worked best. Then she did.

"Gee!" she said. "This seems to be exactly right. I've got them set in high and third."

"Yes," he said, pedaling beside her. "That's the set I use, too."

Elated, she pushed on the pedals and easily moved away from him. He realized what an advantage the ten-speed was. He tried to keep up. He did, but it was work. She glided ahead, he slightly behind watched her smooth legs moving rhythmically up and down, her buttocks smooth over the saddle.

On the long, sloping ride to Ninety-Second Street, they seemed to coast as if in a dream, the ten-speed constantly ahead, he not minding at all. She seemed to know his secret and liked his looking at her. As they cruised along, she glanced back now and then and smiled.

"Marvelous!" she said. "I never knew how much freedom, how wonderful it was to ride one of these. It's so much easier than mine."

"Yes," he said. "Yours is harder to pedal, and it doesn't roll as easily."

"You could go anywhere on this bicycle, and it would never be a problem," she said.

42

"I wonder if she really knows what that means," he thought.

"I can't stop," she called back, "it's too much. Can we go on . . . farther?"

"As far as you like," he answered.

"*Suivez-moi!*" she laughed.

On they went. Sunlight flashed, cut by the shadows of trees. Their legs worked up and down. At slight rises she pulled ahead, but always slowed to wait for him. They now rode in unison, gliding, moving effortlessly, joyously together, the bikes singing over the road as they began a complete circle around Central Park.

They turned onto a small crossway that meanders across the great North Meadow. The meadow rolled away on either side, trees crested the horizon, the sky soared up and up. It was easy for him to stay abreast of her, she did not want to go faster. Wheel to wheel, they glided along. The sunlight seemed to melt the earth beneath them, and they rode suspended. Her T-shirt blew against her good, strong breasts, her lovely legs turned effortlessly. Her small hands clasped the handlebars. She held her chin slightly up, her eyes partly closed, as if seeking a suntan.

"Careful," he said. "You're liable to go right off the end of the Earth."

"I wish I could," she whispered.

The rhythm of their ride grew deeper, stronger. She, lifting her head, every now and then, with her eyes closed. He pedaled strongly. Together they went up a hill. In silhouette, impossible to tell one rider from the other.

They crested a hill, slid down a long slope. Perhaps

43

he had been pedaling harder, he started to pull away.

"Don't leave me," she called.

"No, I won't. Come with me." He held back until she came abreast.

At last they stopped in a little bowl where the road dips and, as if by mutual consent, got off and walked the bikes up a slight rise. Here all was quiet, slightly deserted. The sun came down in great waves over the meadow, and from the hill they could see the cars sparkling along Fifth Avenue, the people moving on bicycles. They themselves were strangely alone, isolated. It was as if they both could look down onto a world conveniently separated from them.

"Great!" she finally said. "But I don't think it's fair for me to be riding your bike. I know mine is a lot harder."

"And, of course, you're so much younger," Stephan said. "And stronger?"

"*Touché*," she said.

They sat beside each other, not saying anything for a while. Almost unconsciously, their hands crept toward one another. Soon Stephan was holding Pia's in his own.

"Nothing quite like it," Pia said.

"No," Stephan agreed, "it wasn't like anything before. But then, when I'm with you nothing ever really is."

He felt her stiffen ever so slightly.

"I wish you wouldn't say things like that."

"Why?" he asked.

"I just wish you wouldn't."

He felt as if he had penetrated some layer that she wished to keep to herself. And yet he could not stop.

"Well, I'm not trying to make it more than it is," he

44

said. "It's something I don't quite understand and, quite frankly, I don't think you do either."

"No," she agreed, "I don't think I do."

"Is it because witches never fall in love?"

"Love? What is that?" she asked. "I'm in love with everything."

"Yes, I think you are. But that's not what I'm talking about and you know it."

Again she was silent. He didn't know whether to try to continue or whether they should get back on their bicycles. She seemed always ready to try to escape.

"You know," he continued, "I never quite feel that you are with me."

"Oh, yes," she answered, "I'm very much with you."

And again he sensed there was something defensive, as if she were trying to put off further questions.

"Will you disappear if I keep on talking?" he asked.

"What do you mean, 'disappear'?"

"I don't quite know myself," he said. "This is the second time something has happened to me in this park. Something I don't quite understand and don't feel is real, and yet I know it is happening."

"The 'second time'?" she asked.

Stephan told her about the rider on the bicycle, his experience on the bench.

"I don't know if all that really happened to me either," he said. "I get the same feeling when I'm with you, a kind of a fantasy."

"Tell me more," she said.

Stephan told about the first time he thought he saw the old bicycle and its rider.

"Tell me about him," she said. "What did he look like?"

"Well, there's not much more," Stephan said. "I

think I've told you all I know. I really can't describe him. I know that it sounds crazy to think you see someone following you on an old-fashioned bicycle, but I guess anything goes in New York. . . ."

"True, true," she said. "Sometimes it's hard to separate reality from fantasy. Why try?"

"Because I feel it has to do with me."

"How?" she asked.

"I don't know. I feel it does. Is it my imagination?" he said. "Have I been imagining the rider? Am I imagining you now?"

"What if you are," she said. "Do you enjoy it?"

"Yes, more than anything for a long, long time."

"Isn't that enough?" she asked.

"I wish it were," he said, "but I'm the kind of person who must have answers to everything."

"Yes, but sometimes there are no answers."

"There you go," he said, "being just as intelligent as I."

"There I go," she said. "Say! Why don't we look for him!"

"Look for him? Where?"

"Maybe he's here in the park."

"Today?"

"Why not?"

"Well, even if he were, how would you find him? There must be a quarter of a million people here." Stephan felt himself becoming more and more defensive, yet he also sensed Pia was baiting him, or at least teasing.

"Listen," she said. "I've got a better idea. Why don't we ride down to the Battery? That's where you saw him first, wasn't it?"

"Yes, but. . . ."

46

"But what? Don't you really want to find him? Maybe if we do, he'll tell us his secret."

"His secret?" Stephan asked. "What secret?"

"Why, the secret everyone is looking for!" With that, she got on her bicycle and pedaled across the grass to the road.

For a moment Stephan was at a loss. He watched her and thought, "Let her go. This is something I don't want to handle, I don't have to handle."

He felt he was being forced into something. And yet, he knew he did not want to lose Pia. He also felt foolish for being unwilling to experience something that he could not completely control. He got on his bike and pedaled after her.

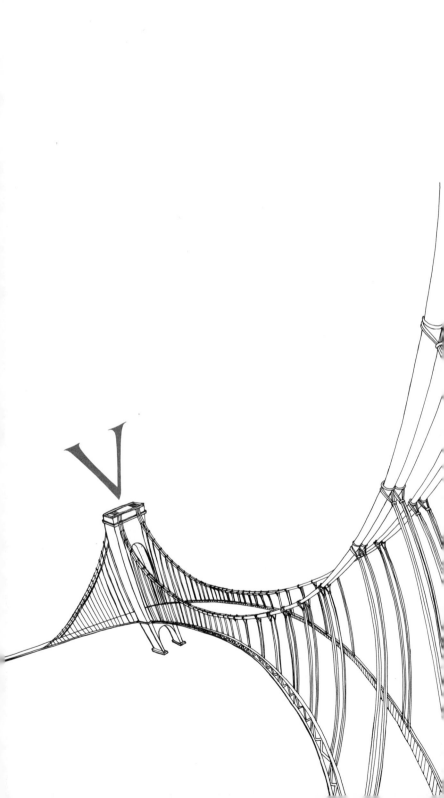

V

Now Pia headed off with an intensity Stephan had not noticed before. It angered him; it shut him out. She was in a world which did not include him. He followed her down the East Drive and out of the park. They sped along Fifth Avenue, the Sunday crowds little more than a blur. She was an excellent rider, obviously used to the city. She knew how to handle the lights at cross-streets, and pedestrians. She never put her foot down; she moved adroitly, circled in and out between automobiles, pushed ahead. Even though Stephan had the faster bicycle, he had difficulty keeping up.

As they went down lower Fifth Avenue, he wanted to call her back. Although he felt foolish for being concerned, it was getting late for a ride to the Battery.

On and on they went through the quiet of deserted streets. Pia worked westward until they found themselves below Soho. They had gone over nine miles, faster than Stephan had ever ridden before.

"Come on," she said. "I know where we can get a beer."

"I thought you wanted to find the cyclist."

"Oh, there's plenty of time," she said. "Let's stop. I'm thirsty again."

They stopped at a small, open-air bar with a raised terrace on Duane Street. They leaned their bicycles against the lower railing and sat on the wood deck, where a young waitress brought them cold bottles of Mexican beer.

They said nothing, but drank gratefully, Stephan, glad that they had stopped, realizing now how thirsty and tired he was, how desperately he had been trying to keep up with Pia.

She sat looking at others with their bicycles leaning the same way. From inside the bar, music rocked the latest tune, everything in concert with the feeling of late afternoon, the music, the young people talking and laughing.

A pleasant Sunday, boys with girls, as pretty as Pia. Yet underneath was a stirring, a kind of apprehension, as if this were an interim, bridge music between two episodes in his life.

As he looked at Pia, he wondered why he could not make his feelings known in the park. Was this only an illusion of having her? She was on some kind of an excursion which seemed to involve herself more than him. Was it simply childish excitement at a new venture? Children often become so consumed they forget about adults. Yet, he knew this was his way of protecting himself. Although it was comforting to him to let someone else take responsibility, he did not know how to handle it.

When the waitress came by they ordered again.

"Marvelous!" Pia said. "It's exactly what I wanted."

He looked at her across the table and said, "So did I."

Her face was slightly flushed and beads of perspiration pearled her upper lip.

"How pretty you look," he said.

"I know," she told him. "I feel pretty. But it's nice to have you tell me."

Stephan wanted the beer, the talk and

the music to go on and on. For that one moment when he told her how pretty she looked they seemed to touch. But even as they sat there he felt her slipping away.

"Hungry?" he asked.

"Yes, a little," she said.

"I wonder," he said, "if there's a place where we could get something to eat?"

"Oh, no. I don't want to do that," she said. "Let's just finish the beer. Then we'll look for your friend."

"My friend?" he said. "I hadn't thought of him that way."

"Well, why don't you?" she said. "Maybe he is."

"How would I know that?" Stephan asked.

"You don't. But is there anything the matter with thinking of him that way, rather than some kind of phantom chasing you?"

"No, I guess not, but thinking won't change my feelings."

"Then I guess we'd better get started," she said, quickly finishing the last of her beer. She bolted down the steps, hardly giving Stephan the chance to pay the waitress, get on his bicycle and follow.

Again the tension. Pia seemed very purposeful. Methodically she covered each block. It was almost as if she knew whom she was looking for.

Stephan still was not willing to believe she knew more than he. Yet there was the nagging suspicion she had some purpose that went beyond what she communicated. Stephan hated himself for being so paranoid. Why should he be suspicious? Wasn't she trying to help him? Why did he feel that she was forcing him? Was it true? Or was he simply holding back from the excitement of being alive?

After they had covered several blocks, Pia said, "Stephan, why don't we split up? I'll try to cover as much as I can below Wall Street and you look above. And . . . "

"And what?" Stephan said, knowing he sounded irritated. "Suppose you find him. Or I do. How will we let the other know?"

"Why? Is that so important? We're not trying to capture him. If we see him, won't that be enough?"

Stephan accepted.

They decided on a place to meet and started out. Stephan was relieved to be alone; it enabled him to gain some perspective. He wondered why he felt so much more at ease now than when he was riding with Pia.

Now the sun sank lower, heavy shadows fell between buildings. Momentarily, Stephan was lost in their interplay, finding a sense of peace simply riding through them. At last, he realized it was going to become more difficult to recognize even Pia, let alone a strange bicyclist. He decided to go back to the flower shop where they had agreed to meet and wait.

Once there, he leaned his bicycle against the building and lit a cigarette. He relaxed, bathing in that luxury of time when he had nothing to do. But before long his natural anxiousness reasserted itself. He peered down the darkening streets for Pia.

Nothing.

Only the lights of oncoming automobiles glowing in the heavying dusk. In her enthusiasm it could be easy for Pia to get carried away.

He could no longer contain himself. He decided to cruise around the block and perhaps meet her. He did, but she did not appear. He then began to widen the circles, looking not for the bicyclist, but for her. Each time he came back to his starting point he hoped she would be waiting. Yet, each time he somehow knew she would not be there. And she was not.

He felt more anxious, and silly. Only ten or fifteen minutes had passed. Should he wait, or extend his search? What would happen if she returned and he was not there? Would she wait?

All this went through his head as he pedaled faster and faster through the now-empty streets, not concerned about the bicyclist, only Pia. Several times he saw a cyclist and was elated. But it was not she.

He did not know what to do. Should he give up, go back to his apartment? Perhaps Pia would phone him. He could call her. He hated the thought of hearing the telephone ring and ring and ring in her apartment with no answer.

As soon as he turned into one street and saw no one, he was in a rush to get to the next block. He was both angry and panicked. Angry with Pia, angry with himself.

It was growing darker, the streets emptier. In a few minutes Stephan would have no chance of finding Pia at all.

He made one last pass and then circled back to the flower store, lonelier now by the light of the street lamp on its iron gates. It would have been foolish for Pia to wait, and dangerous.

Stephan knew he had lost her. She must have left. It would not have been unlike her—or so he thought—to have met some friends and completely forgotten about him. He had a momentary flash of fury as he imagined her upstairs in one of the nearby lofts, laughing, talking with friends, drinking wine.

Almost certainly there would be paintings and an easel standing in the background.

He realized his fantasizing only fed his frustration, and decided to return to his apartment. He resolved, however, to ride to her block on Fourteenth Street, although he did not know her building.

Riding uptown, he felt more relaxed. Going to Fourteenth Street was probably pointless, but somehow it eased his anxiety. He was beginning to feel tired, drained, and looked forward to getting back to his own apartment.

He knew Pia lived between Eighth and Ninth Avenues, a strangely quiet block with old brownstones, trees and a church. Even as he turned into her block, he knew it too would be empty. The ride was a gesture. But there, on a pair of stairs of a brownstone directly across from the church, her bicycle leaning on the railing, was Pia.

Even in the twilight he knew it was she. He pedaled up to her, not knowing quite what to say. Pia, instead of her usual spontaneity, neither shouted nor jumped up, but instead held out her hand to him. He took it and sat down beside her.

He did not know how long they sat. A few minutes, perhaps, but Stephan wanted the moment to go on forever, her hair against his cheek, the damp feel of her bare arm as her hand cradled in his, her quiet breathing.

At last she spoke.

"I was foolish," she said. "I don't know what made me do it. I just felt angry with you."

"Angry with me?"

"Yes, you just sat there drinking your beer. Like some wise sphinx. I think if I hadn't run off the porch you would have stayed there forever, immobilized."

"Did I really look that way?"

"Yes, you did. I knew that you wanted to find that cyclist and yet you just sat there, refusing to do anything."

"That was wrong."

"But I was wrong, too. I should not have forced you. Oh, Stephan, let's not try to force each other to do something we don't want to do ever again."

"I promise."

And before either of them quite knew what was happening, they were kissing. Pia was crying and Stephan felt like crying, too. Strange how this girl made him feel so human, so easily.

"Come," she whispered, and stood up. Taking his hand, she led him down the steps and into her apartment. They parked their bikes in the hall, and without turning on the lights felt their way into her bedroom. He was aware she was taking her clothes off and he was doing the same. It all happened so naturally, he felt as if he were observing someone else.

But once their clothes were off and their arms around each other, nothing was more real.

Pia's eyes were closed, small musical moans came from her throat. She was passive, quieter than he expected. But then they grew together and her quietude enveloped him. He found a willingness and strength he never knew he possessed.

Afterward, they drifted off to sleep. How long, Stephan did not know.

Toward morning Stephan awoke to find Pia lying against him, looking at him.

"No fair," he said. "It is I who should be looking at you."

56

"I like to look at you. You are the most beautiful man in the world."

Again he did not know what to say.

"You don't need him," she said.

"Him?"

"The bicyclist."

"Our nemesis?" he asked.

"There is no nemesis. No bicyclist."

"How do you know?"

"I don't know, Stephan. I just feel."

"But why did you insist we go look for him, even separate so we'd have a better chance of finding him?"

"Oh, Stephan, I knew you wouldn't find him. I just hoped you would find yourself."

"Myself?"

"Yes, that's all there has ever been, ever will be."

He pulled her close to him.

"Where did you get so much knowledge?" he asked.

"Witches go on feelings."

She allowed herself to be drawn into his arms once again. He stroked her hair, but even as the quiet and peace ran over them he felt her drifting away.

At last she disentangled her arm from him and sat up. She uncurled in preparation to say something and the movement pacified rather than excited him.

"You once told me," she said, "you want to know everything, tie it down, label it. You had to find the cyclist even though you knew he really does not exist. You're too intelligent not to know that."

"And if I am left only with myself?" he asked. "Then what?"

"Find yourself," she answered. Then she reached over and kissed him.

"Now you must go," was the last thing she said.

He got up and dressed. They simply touched hands, and he let himself out of the apartment, pushing the bicycle ahead of him.

Out on the street he felt very much at peace.

"This is how you must feel when you are loved," he thought. "No," he continued, "this is how you feel when you know you can love yourself."

Once again, as he pedaled home, he knew the wheels did not touch the ground.

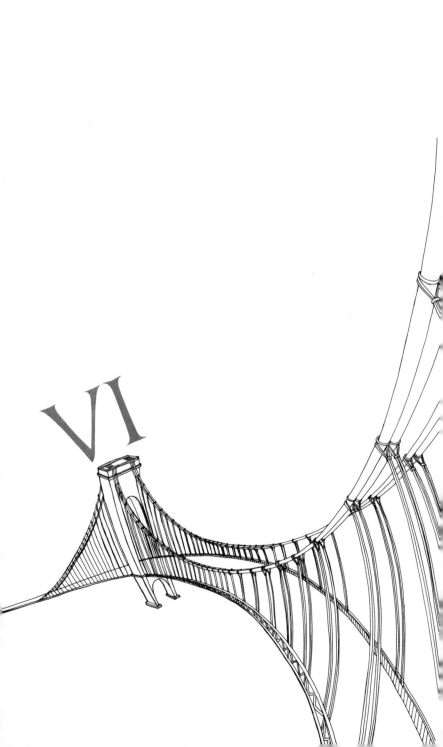

VI

Later, that evening, as he sat in the darkened apartment with only the lights from the street reflecting on the rims of the ten-speed, he felt as if he were emerging from a dream. Part of him wanted to go back to sleep, another to waken. For a few minutes he sat in limbo. He knew what had happened with Pia had been real. What surrounded the event, however, was still quixotic.

Was she right? Should he give up the idea of ever finding the other cyclist? Did it matter? What would it prove if he did? To Stephan, the possibility he was being followed meant something. But what?

Stephan knew he could go on for weeks, perhaps years, trying to unravel a secret he could never fully understand.

A new discovery was needed—a discovery that comes from looking ahead. It was time to go on. To go back only meant eternal self-examination, retribution piled on retribution, Pyrrhic victories that only wrapped the old Stephan more tightly into himself.

To go on. But where?

"Why, to the moon, of course," a voice within Stephan seemed to say.

He felt a tremendous sense of relief, elation. Everything seemed to fall into place. He regretted there was no one to share this with. How marvelous for another to have seen what he had seen, to know what a bicycle could do, what anyone could do! But he realized it was something each person must find out for himself.

At first he thought it might be a good idea to try an

experimental flight to prove out his theory. A flight to the moon was quite a risk. How could he dare?

Yet some inner momentum had caught him up. "Experimental" flights were merely rationalizations, reachings back. The decision to go ahead had been made. He must recognize it.

"Go on," he said. "Do it."

He knew he could wait no longer. Summer was rapidly drawing to a close. The soft warmth of August engulfed New York. The heat that sometimes is so heavy now had an effulgence, was warm and clear, not oppressive. People remarked about the curious quality of the air. Men and boys, tanned, walked beautiful women along Fifth Avenue.

"This is the time to go," he thought. "A time of happiness."

But first he must settle with Sherman, perhaps the thing he hated most. For almost a year now, his fat, amicable partner had put up with Stephan's absences almost with a sense of hurt. But this was different.

The very next day, Stephan got to the office early. But Sherman, as usual, was there ahead of him. Sherman was always there, ahead.

"Hey, stranger?" Sherman called cordially. "You're just in time. The Triangle job came through and I'm meeting with them this afternoon. I'll need some roughs before we can go into the final specs. And listen, while I'm down there, talk to the printer. I know they're jammed up and we better schedule some press time."

He would have gone on, but Stephan held up his hands in surrender.

"How about letting me get a cup of coffee?" he said.

"Oh, sure, sure. Margaret, get Stevie a cup of coffee and get me one, too, will you? Do me a favor, Stevie, hand me those mechanicals."

Margaret, Sherman's secretary and constant shadow, winked at Stephan. She was already bringing the coffee.

"You have a few minutes?" Stephan said.

"Sure, sure. Just let me make a phone call—one, I promise you. Margaret, do me a favor, get this number for me, please. Then no more calls."

Stephan drank his coffee while Sherman made his call. Sitting there, he felt more like an employee than a partner. When Sherman finished, he hung up, looked at Stephan as if he were going to say something, but Stephan held up his hand.

"No, Sherman, wait."

As quickly and directly as he could he told Sherman he wanted out. When he finished, Sherman stared hard at him.

"Well, if that's what you want," he said. "Have you thought about taking a vacation, a real vacation, instead of pissing around the edges?"

"No, Sherman, no vacation. Out."

"What are you going to do? Go on your own? Got another offer? You're lucky, with your talent, there's always someone who will need you. Me, I'm just a poor slob salesman."

"You're not just a salesman. You know that. No, I don't know what I'm going to do, but I need some time, and it's not fair to you—or to me—to keep it dragging on this way."

He wondered what Sherman would have said if he had told him the real reason.

"Okay, but you've got to help me through the Triangle job. After all, you're still my partner."

So there was to be no trip to the moon. At least, not now. Stephan realized he was just going to have to sit down and do the Triangle job.

"Okay," he said. "We'll get it out."

"Good."

Stephan started back to his own office. Sherman was already on the phone when Stephan turned.

"Sherman," he said, "just for once, try 'we're partners' instead of 'my partner.'"

"What did you say?" Sherman asked, putting his hand over the phone.

"Nothing," Stephan answered, and went back to work. Once again Sherman had won, as Stephan knew he would. The job went on solidly for almost forty-eight hours without a break. But when he was finished, and finally stepped out of the office into the late evening, he felt freer than he had ever felt before.

It took him another night of good sound sleep to get over all his tiredness. He slept as he never had before. On a quiet morning, the first week of August, he awakened feeling calm and refreshed. He knew that this was the day.

He called Dorothy that evening. Although she did not try to understand why he must see her then, she agreed to meet him in front of their old apartment, where she still lived, within the hour.

Stephan was ready.

He put on a pair of dungarees, his moccasins, an open-necked shirt, and white sweater. He did not know if there were any crazy drivers among the stars, but at least they could see him. He wheeled the bicycle out of the apartment, closed the door and left a note for Mrs. Applebaum, his next-door neighbor.

"I have gone for a slight trip," it said. "If you don't hear from me in the next week or so. . . ." And then he gave instructions what to do about his keys.

By 7:15 he was on West End Avenue just as his wife came out of the building.

She looked like a little fairy to him. Petite, dark-haired, with that striking ability to dress; so under-stated, so dramatic, something that never ceased to thrill him. Even now, in the casualness of summer, she shone effortlessly. She saw him coming, waved.

The street hung in a kind of silence. Few people. Even the sound of automobiles was damped.

As he rode up she said, "You look very professional with your white sweater tied around you. Do you think you really need it this evening?"

"I may need it a little later. Sometimes it gets a little chilly."

"Always so conservative," she chided, but ever so gently.

"Yes, I guess I'll never learn."

They talked about little nothings, each cautiously inquiring about the other.

Finally he said, "I was in the country the other day."

"Oh," she said.

"Yes, I was talking with Dave and he mentioned that you've been going to Boston weekends. Someone you met at Club Med."

"Dave was always a good gossip," she said.

"Do you mind he told me? He didn't intend to. I wasn't asking. You must understand this . . . really! We were talking about something else and he men-

66

tioned they had spoken to you, and in the course of the conversation you told him you were dating this man from Boston."

"It's true," she said. "I guess there's no way Dave would not have told you. Yes, yes, I do see someone."

He wanted to ask, "Do you go every weekend?" He knew it was none of his business.

"Nice?"

"Yes, a nice guy. In certain ways he's very much like you, and in other ways there's absolutely no resemblance."

"How do you feel about him?" he asked.

"I like being liked."

"Yes," he said, "I know. It's good when it comes easily, isn't it?"

She seemed to wince, but she did not back off from the fact that she was proud, happy that someone could like her. With no reservations, no conditions.

"And what about you?" she asked.

"Well," he said, "I'm not going to Boston."

"Dave and Lil tell me that you had someone up to the country a few weeks ago."

"I did, but I'm not seeing her any longer."

"Why? Didn't you like her?"

"Yes, I liked her."

"Then why don't you see her?"

"I only said I liked her."

"And how did she feel about you?"

"She liked me, too."

"Well, then," she said.

"Well, then, it means we simply liked one another. There were others, at least in her life. I'm somewhere else now."

"Where?" she asked.

"As a matter of fact," he said, "I'm on my way to the moon."

"Oh," she said. "When?" She was not surprised. It was the type of statement he always made.

"This evening."

"This evening? Well, it's a good night for it."

"Yes, I thought so, too," he answered. "It's warm, pleasant."

"Is that all you're going to wear, just your sweater?"

"Yes, I'm not sure I'll need it, but just in case I'll have it with me."

"Good idea. How long do you think you'll be gone?"

"I don't know," he said. "I've never been to the moon."

"I know that," she said. "Do you think it will take long?"

"I can't really say."

"I can't really say," she repeated. "You are always so evasive when someone asks you a direct question."

"I know, but this time I'd really like to answer you. I just don't know."

She knew he meant it.

"This is the first time," she said, "I've ever heard you say something so openly. It's good."

He smiled.

"I know," he said. "It's not like me at all, is it?"

"No, not true. You usually know what you want to do, you're just afraid to say it."

"Curious you should know that now," he said.

"I think I've always known it. It's just that I can say it now."

68

For the first time in a long while he realized they were both reaching out to one another. Not to reclaim, but to tell each other it had not all been bad. But, if they both knew where they were going, the road signs did not make the parting easier.

At least, he knew he must leave.

"Trips to the moon probably take a long time," he said. "I think I had better start."

She smiled. The same smile she smiled the very first time he left.

"Take care of yourself. I want to hear about it all when you come back."

"Oh, yes," he said. "You'll be the first I want to tell."

"Take care of yourself," she said. Her eyes brimmed.

He leaned forward over the handlebars and kissed her on the forehead. It had always been their own special way of saying hello. And goodbye.

Riding down West End Avenue, he remembered. The many nights in summer, autumn, winter, fall, when he walked Sam here. To Broadway, Sundays, to get the *Times*, to Riverside Park to play in the snow. He remembered how he and Dorothy walked to the movies, the Midtown, Symphony, Thalia. Remembered.

"I wouldn't have missed a minute of it," he thought. That helped.

Gradually, his nostalgia and melancholy left. West End Avenue was but another street in that city where all streets intrigued him on. The trees on either side, the old ladies who crossed unconcernedly against the lights, the kids on delivery bikes with the aluminum boxes that thumped as they jumped curbs. Roof lights on the taxis, lights in the apartments. Sounds. He felt he and the city shared a love, as he did with Dorothy.

He turned off West End to Riverside Drive and headed north toward the George Washington Bridge. In a few minutes he was almost under it. The great skeleton of steel towers stretched up and seemed to disappear into the sky. Slender filaments of cable webbed the deck in place. Closer and closer the bridge loomed, large, fearsome. It towered so high over Stephan, he became dizzy looking up. For some reason it seemed to threaten to topple over on him.

Fly from that bridge? Impossible! The high arc over the sullen waters below yawned and terrified him.

"Go back," he thought.

Back? To what? To all the old patterns that had trapped him before, that would hold him forever if he went back now?

He must go on. If it were true, he was learning to love himself, he must go on.

"This time I will not turn away from myself," he thought as he pedaled up the ramp to the sidewalk on the top deck of the bridge. The roadway was like a runway, lit on either side. His take-off strip.

Stephan did not dare look up. He knew the towers loomed above him. To his left, Manhattan glowed. On the road beside him, traffic roared by. He wondered if anyone watched, but he did not care. He shifted into high, stood up over the pedals and began to pump, hard.

Now the bike moved swiftly, the tires sang on the pavement, and he felt the bite of his wheels as they cut his path. He knew he was pedaling as skillfully as any bicyclist ever had before. Bike and he were one. Surely this is the way the great cyclists must have felt in those moments when they knew triumph was theirs. They were winning. This was a win!

He was at the center of the bridge. Now!

At the point where the curve of the support cables meet the roadway, Stephan pulled back sharply, aimed the bike out, away from the bridge. The bike hung for a split second, then lifted, shot out over the railing. Momentum gave him a tremendous shove and he shot up, up, up, up, high above the shining necklace of lights that outlines the bridge. Up into the penumbra of singing space.

In the air!

"I'm flying!" he exulted. "Someone should see me. Dorothy! Pia! *World!* I'm flying!"

He pulled away from the great symphony of the bridge. He breathed easily now, and his heart had stopped pounding. A cool, gentle breeze dried the perspiration on his neck and temples. He opened and closed his hands on the handlebars. All the tension left him.

To prove he was really in control, he swung away from the path over the river and did a smooth, graceful figure eight around the cheerful little red light that sits atop the Cloisters. Now he knew what he would do: first a long, leisurely trip over Manhattan, and then, to the moon.

The deep, dark greens of Fort Tryon and Inwood Park slanted away from him, gentle and cushiony. The bike rose a little more.

At this point absolutely no resistance, and as he pedaled along, the bike bit into the air, moving with crispness and ease. When he felt he had pedaled enough, he coasted. Below him, Inwood, sliced by Dyckman Street. Ahead, Washington Heights. Off to his right and slightly below, the George Washington Bridge stretched across to Jersey, its necklace celebrated the Hudson. The river itself faintly luminescent, glowing.

As he looked south, the whole city took on an irridescence, a glow fog that radiated and pulsated with life of its own. He pedaled over Morningside Heights, looking down to the campus of Columbia and the dark green separating the Heights from Harlem.

In Harlem, gentle row after gentle row of brownstones were warm and soft. "What a lovely neighborhood," he thought. "Look at those majestic houses. It's the only place in this city with its own dignity."

The summer breeze touched his face. He was not a bit cold. In fact, the light wool sweater tied over his shoulders was just right.

He stayed over the West Side because that was always his favorite part of New York. Sometimes going higher, sometimes dropping lower.

The big apartments were honeycombed with light. In one apartment he saw a man entirely naked watch television as he stood in the middle of his living room, pensively scratching his behind.

He pedaled easily along, seeing the outline of the Dakota as it cut into the darker area of Central Park, the beads of light that wound around from the drives, sensual curves against the rigid grid of Manhattan. The hotel signs on Central Park South glowed in an arching rainbow of light that arabesqued along the straight, dark edge of the park. He wondered what was playing at the Paris as he continued on down over Times Square. He was too high to hear the horns or the voices of the thousands and thousands of people.

"I wonder if they know they look like bugs lit up from the inside," he thought.

South of Forty-Second Street, the city darkened. The Empire State Building stood up tall, straight, surrounded by the dark. After the incandescence of Times Square, it was quiet and peaceful.

"This must be something like it is in space," he thought. "In the center, darkness, and at the edges, light." He coasted over Herald Square, faintly lit, nothing to compare with the brilliance and near sense of heat that rose from Times Square.

He continued on south, over Chelsea, across Fourteenth Street, and over the Village. Sixth Avenue met Eighth Street where the fruit stand and the flower market glowed ever so brightly. Stephan remembered how many times he had walked by there. Though he rarely bought anything, he always felt a sense of possession, as if the fruit and the flowers were a sort of tribute to him and to the city.

Once past the Village, Manhattan darkened even more. He sailed over the warehouses—his warehouses—and the same aromas that greeted him when he first rode through seemed now to rise and surround him. How long ago that first ride seemed!

Ahead, the towers of the World Trade Center, his final beacon on Earth. His only regret was that there was no one at the tip of the Battery to wish him "*Bon voyage!*" or to go with him. Ah! if only he had company. How complete!

What Stephan did not know was that he *did* have company. Just behind him trotted a big white dog.

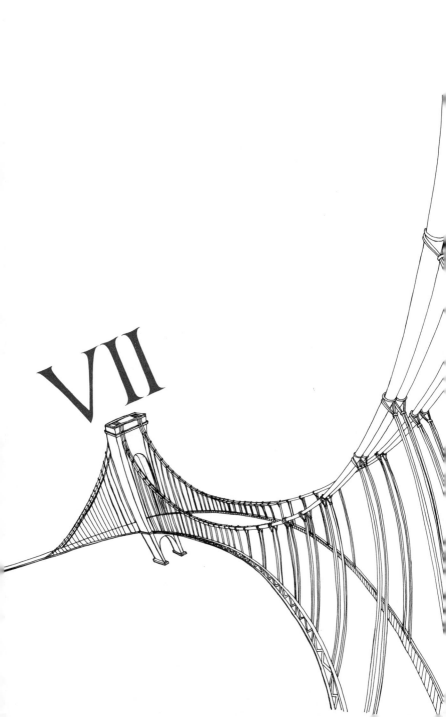

VII

As Stephan pedaled, the curve of the Verrazzano Bridge stood out bold and clear. He pulled back, sharply, climbed more steeply. There in the harbor, several ships, waiting to be berthed, sent out pools of light. He concentrated on pedaling and, as the dark vault of the bridge loomed closer and closer, he realized that he would soon swing above and over it.

As he rode, he felt there was light and music coming from the city. It was as if all the millions of New Yorkers had stopped and were standing there, waving their hats, cheering him, singing. A man sitting reading a newspaper on the East Side, someone else taking his children out for ice cream, lines of people on Third Avenue waiting to get into the Baronet, Cinema 2 and 3. Somewhere, somehow, a part of them saw, and cheered, and were glad. All over Manhattan they were glad.

He did a few daring curves, not turning the wheels, but laying from side to side, so that the bike swept in graceful arcs, on and up. He no longer felt the sense of the music or the light from the city. Below him was a dark, warm presence that took on a luminosity of its own he knew was the Earth.

"I wonder if I'm going at the speed of light," he thought. "The Earth seems to be disappearing away from me so quickly."

Now he rose in a sense of exaltation and triumph. "This is *my* winning," he thought.

He remembered the first time he had taken the bicycle out and timorously ridden down First Avenue. How he had gone through the Village, had been amazed at his bravado in going down toward the World Trade Center. All those speculative first attempts.

By now, the Earth was but a small dot behind him, a small, silver-blue pearl, rapidly being wreathed in mist and fog.

"Where is the moon?" he thought.

He felt as if he were rising up through a bubble bath of stars, lights scintillating around him, glowing tiny dots, comets, meteors turning in graceful arcs and spirals, fireworks that triumphantly lit his way upward. He knew he passed great stars, wished he could remember their names.

"I really should have made a more serious study of the Universe," he thought. But not knowing was knowing; he was part of it all. He realized that he was climbing up through the Milky Way, and knew that he was rocketing through the Pleiades, past Taurus, past giant, full-blown red stars, and dying white ones. "But they will be reborn again in some other kind of matter," he thought.

Space opened out in a breadth of ecstasy; even though it was dark at the outmost perimeters, there was a sense of light around him all the time. He felt neither cold nor warm. Everything seemed just right. Curiously, the light seemed ever-increasing although it was still dark.

"There's something marvelous about our shining in the dark," he thought.

How long he traveled, he did not know. Occasionally, he pedaled, but for the most part he coasted. It did not seem to matter. He was not even sure that when he shifted it was easier to pedal. He just did it to amuse himself and to show the stars that he could do things, too. The bike moved smoothly, the wheels turned easily. He seemed to hiss through space. On and on, through the crust of the Milky Way and into a darkness soft and velvety—a relief after the brilliance and kaleidoscope of color he had just experienced.

Now it was quieter, peaceful. He was not sure what arc he followed, but he was not concerned. He knew that another *nebula* was far out beyond the Milky Way, probably the Andromeda Galaxy. Sooner or later, he would come to it.

Despite the ecstasy of discovery, Stephan felt he wanted something more. He knew he did not want to just drift aimlessly in space.

But, of course, the moon! He had been so immersed in all that was new, he had forgotten he had intended to go to the moon. And, curiously, with that realization, a large mass began to drift toward him from the horizon. The moon? He could not be sure, but he turned the bicycle and began pedaling toward it.

He had no way of calculating time and space. He wished he had studied the movements of the stars more. He was really quite unprepared. The minutest fraction of error and he could miss the moon, go on pedaling through space forever.

"But wait," he thought. "Why am I holding myself back with rules and regulations? Surely I can go beyond that. If I believed I could make the bicycle fly, then I can make it to the moon. Rules and regulations are *not* limits, only places to begin."

78

The glowing mass seemed to beckon to him. He knew he was going in the right direction.

"How nice," he thought, "to have a purpose, even if it does not always turn out the way you expect."

As he rode on, he sensed that not only would he find the moon, but something more. What that "something" would be, he was not sure. A little tremor, not of fear, but of anticipation, tingled in his spine.

Now this feeling mingled with another.

He looked back. Nothing. But the feeling of inevitability, of something coming to him, continued. Only now he realized that he was looking for it as much as whatever it was was looking for him.

As he drew nearer he was more aware of a bigger force pulling him. Gravity? Perhaps. He felt some trepidation. Once he landed would he be able to leave? Why not? He had been able to leave the Earth. Now it was more important to find out what beckoned him to the moon.

As he drew near, the sky filled with a silvery glow that permeated the space around him. The glow deepened, seemed to become more solid, as if Stephan were moving through a molten sea. As the atmosphere thickened, he felt suspended, and momentarily considered turning away.

How could he be certain he actually headed for the moon? Perhaps he was being trapped in some foreign galaxy or planet, doomed to spin and spin forever in a silver haze, his transparency finally amalgamated with the nothingness of space.

So be it. He made the choice to go ahead. He no longer could see. Shortly he felt a soft thud under the wheels, and knew he had landed. On the moon?

Then, magically, the fog lifted. Space no longer curved, but stretched out ahead in a desert of craters, rocks, sand and dust, all in a neutral gray that looked neither alive nor dead, but as if it had been asleep forever.

He put one foot down gingerly.

He expected billows of dust to rise, but instead it was as if he stepped onto some hard-packed beach. He got off the bicycle and stretched. He set the kickstand and walked a few yards away. The ten-speed looked no more incongruous than pictures of spaceships sitting on the moon. Neither belonged.

He tried to get some sort of bearing.

Everything looked the same. Perhaps he had landed on some burned-out star, or even on an insignificant asteroid. So what? He was somewhere. That had to count. Then, suddenly, he knew.

Over his shoulder, far larger than he could have imagined, glowed the Earth. It looked like a giant blue marble wreathed in mist. No doubt about it: Earth! Even through the mists he made out continents. Yes! There they were, oceans, islands, and, as he watched, North America turned into view.

"And I thought I was getting old and needed stronger glasses," Stephan thought as the elation welled within. Not at all! Everything was sharp and clear as if held under a powerful magnifying glass.

He sat down with his knees pulled up, tucked under his chin, and stared at the Earth in much the same way as he had stared at waves breaking on the beach, held in the hypnotic movement that leads to all kinds of dreams.

"It's strange," Stephan thought. "I may be looking down on the very streets where once I rode and walked."

He could imagine himself back there now, walking the streets, alone, wistful, wishing someone were with him.

"I wonder if someday I'll look up and see this cold, distant moon, and think, 'Once I sat up there, alone, and looked down here.' I wonder if I will still be alone."

He did not know how long he sat, but gradually he began to realize, or sense, he was not by himself. Someone, some thing else was with him.

He stood up. He did not feel frightened; rather, interested. Whatever it was did not seem ominous. He looked around. He felt he was being watched, guarded. The bicycle stood where he had left it. Should he get back on it and scout around? Perhaps, if necessary, fly away?

Casually, he brushed the dust from the seat of his pants and continued to look. Still nothing. Whoever or whatever watched was very careful not to be seen himself. Could he be wrong? Was it simply the overall strangeness? No. He was positive he was being watched.

He strolled leisurely to the bike, put his hands on the handlebars and prepared to mount. He pushed back the kickstand and rolled the bike forward, his left foot on the pedal. He shoved hard and swung his right leg up and over the back wheel as the bike got under way.

As Stephan stood up on the pedals, he sighted a slight rise in the ground just ahead of him, higher

81

than eye level. Rounding the hillock, ears pulled back, eyes squinched together as they always were when he made joyful recognition, was Sam!

The tail wagged slowly. Sam was never foolishly spontaneous. He waited for recognition from Stephan. But Stephan could only stare.

Is this who had been following all this time? Had the unknown cyclist somehow miraculously transformed into the great white dog? Impossible? Of all the fantastic events that had crowded into Stephan's life since he left the planet Earth, he still was not quite prepared for this metamorphosis.

But there stood Sam, mouth slightly open, panting warmly with what could only be described as a smile. Sam, not ten yards from Stephan, with a look that said, "Of course it's me. You certainly recognize me, don't you?"

Stephan could bear it no longer. He got off the bike and ran to Sam. Who cared about facts or explanations. Sam! And as Stephan rushed up, the great white dog slowly reared, rising to an imperial five feet, and planted his forepaws on Stephan's shoulders. Now Stephan had him in his arms, really felt him. He ran his hands down the silky ears. The dog let soft, rolling growls ripple from deep in his chest. Sam never kissed, that was for little dogs, but he did lay his muzzle against Stephen. Stephan gently lowered the dog and knelt beside him.

"Sam, is it really you? What are you doing here, old buddy? How great you look!" Stephan's throat tightened, tears were hot in his eyes. He felt it all to be so unreal that if he hugged Sam too tightly the dog would disappear.

"Accept this," something told him. If only here on

the moon this could take place, accept it. The absolute joy of being together again was enough.

Sam responded.

Stretched out on the ground with his forefeet out in front of him, his bottom still high in the air, he rolled over with a terrific thud and pawed angel's wings in the silvery beach. Stephan rubbed his belly. Sam bounded up and dashed about, puppylike, throwing up clouds of sand, barking in unmitigated joy.

He watched the Great Pyrenees roll over on his back, the great tongue extended mischievously, that wild look in his eyes. Stephan had to match Sam's joy with his own.

He ran to his bicycle and got on, shouting, "Come on, Sam! Come on!"

Sam leaped to his feet. In a few huge bounds he was ahead of Stephan. Both he and Stephan became airborne once again, gravity a plaything of outer space.

The two of them bounced up and down as if they rode giant pogo sticks. A quick kiss to the surface of the moon followed by marvelous arcing loops. They touched down for moments only to zoom back off in graceful curves, almost in slow motion. They were in a beautiful celestial waltz where the very rhythm of the music buoyed them up, throwing them in joyous arcs higher and higher.

They dove and rose, arabesquing around each other, now one the pursuer, now the other. And it was not gravity that set them free, but joy.

"We made it, Sam," Stephan cried. "We made it to the moon!"

In a deep, baritone bark, Sam trumpeted back.

Stephan considered settling down on the moon so as not to tire the dog. But this was the magnificent animal he had been in his prime, tireless, powerful, patient, not the Sam of old age.

After the initial symphony of movement, Sam was content to trot along in his space-consuming lope that made it necessary for Stephan to pedal just to keep up. And Sam wanted to go on and on.

Now it was easy for Stephan to remember fondly how exasperated he had often become with Sam. Especially when, on those cold winter nights, Sam had wanted to continue his walks long after Stephan was ready to return to Dorothy and the warmth of their apartment.

As he pedaled along, Stephan could not help thinking how, in retrospect, those characteristics of people and events which were once so aggravating become so nostalgic and endearing through the distillation of time.

Yes, it was time to go on. Together, he and Sam would canvass the prairies of space, explore the reaches of the Pleiades, race past Taurus, see Sirius, Arcturus, and Betelgeuse.

They moved in unison, man and dog. Sam in his easy lope. Stephan pedaling easily, effortless. Quieter now, they sped through space, played hide and seek with tiny asteroids, rode with proper respect past giant galaxies and stars. Could they have been seen, Stephan was certain they would have looked like a beautiful, double-plumed comet that trailed light and happiness across the sky.

Now was the time to head for that far-off galaxy, Andromeda. He had Sam; their energy boundless; time endless. They could wander through space for-

ever. Go beyond Andromeda, if they chose. Stephan felt no need to hurry. All was time; all was peace.

As they cruised along, he thought about Dorothy and Pia. He wondered what they would have felt had they been along.

Sam traveled ahead, occasionally he disappeared, wreathed in mist. And at times it seemed they were going in separate ways, parallel but separate, each in his own world, left to his own thoughts and dreams.

As they rode on, Stephan began to wonder about Pia's adjuration to forget the phantom bicyclist. There seemed to be no real need to find him, to solve the mystery that still, in some small part of Stephan's mind, nagged for a solution. Had it all been his imagination? Had he really seen the cyclist? Even that day in the park, now so far away? He could not be sure, since most of the time his eyes had been closed. Why? What was there he had been afraid to see? Or was Pia right? Perhaps it had only been a fantasy of his and fantasy can often trap you more than reality.

No! That was not what Pia meant. Suddenly he realized that she had been trying to tell him not to feel guilty about dreaming, it's marvelously human. The trick is to know you are doing it—and still enjoy it.

And that was it! That was Pia's real witchery—the witchery of life! That part of ourselves that keeps reaching out, knowing no barriers—or fears—that comes only from an inner confidence and security and says wherever we go, however we reach, we'll be okay. Even if we don't know where the cutting edge of experience will take us, somehow we will find a way. It is only when we bind ourselves with parameters, and rules, rigid patterns, that we throw ourselves against the walls of our personal dungeons, and howl against demons that mock us from the other side of the bars. But no one has locked us in. Only ourselves. The demons wait in the dark—like phantom bicyclists—only as long as we insist on staying in the dark.

Stephan felt a great surge of energy. He must go back, tell the world. No, not tell, *live!* His joy was so great, so uncontainable, he knew instantly he wanted to get back, to return to Earth, to live in those limitless reaches of space that could be anywhere. Earth, sky, within himself.

But how?

He looked ahead for Sam. He had disappeared! No, there he was, far ahead, a vague white dot that Stephan could hardly see. He pedaled faster, almost desperately. The harder he tried to catch up, the farther behind he seemed to fall. He tried to call to Sam, even more desperately now. He was certain the Great Pyrenees was too far away to hear. And then a strange thing started to happen. The bicycle began to lose altitude. Not perceptibly, in fact so little that Stephan told himself it was only his imagination. But no, slowly but surely, not only was he losing ground to Sam, but the bicycle also definitely steepened its descent. Once again he leaned back, as he had done so often before, trying to get the bike to zoom up. He tried harder. No results. Sam was fast disappearing. Once again he called. He thought he saw Sam pause, but was not sure.

And then, to Stephan's terror, he realized that some hideous transmutation had taken place. He no longer rode his ten-speed, but instead was astride the uncomfortable iron saddle of an antique two-wheeler, heavy, ponderous, old. Unbelievable! He could not understand what had happened. The iron handlebars were frightfully cold in his hands. He had the dizzying feeling he was about to fall off.

Then, the bike wheeled over and plunged in a cyclonic rush toward Earth.

At that moment, Dorothy, in bed with her lover, sat up, awakened from a deep sleep. Her heart pounded wildly. The man beside her stirred and put his hand on her arm.

"What is it, honey?" he asked.

"I don't know. I felt I was falling."

"It was a dream," he answered quietly.

"But it was so real."

"Yes, it sometimes is. More real than being awake. Try to sleep."

He put his arms around her.

He was probably right, Dorothy thought, but she was not sure.

At almost the same time, in the Village, Pia, walking with a friend, tripped and would have fallen if he had not caught her.

"You all right?" he asked.

"Yes, I tripped," she said.

But instead of looking down, she stared up at the sky.

Stephan fell, helplessly.

Just before he started to plunge down, he thought he heard himself scream. He hoped Sam heard.

Down he plunged. The roar of space filled his ears. His eyes teared. For a moment he thought he had been thrown clear and was falling free. His stomach tightened. Wind shrieked in his ears. He wanted to cry, to scream. Vaguely, he thought he saw the giant, dark towers of the George Washington Bridge, ominous, powerful, looming behind him. Below, black waters rushed toward him, would soon swallow him up.

That was it! It had all been a dream. He was still falling from the bridge. The bike had never made it. Fool! Ass! He was going to die. Die!

But no. After the first shock of the fall, he realized he was still on the old bicycle. Incongruous! Moments before he was certain he was plunging alone, through some frightening shaft of space, but instead he remained seated.

His heart still pounded. His mouth was dry and he could not get his breath. Under him the bike felt cumbersome, unmanageable. But he held on.

He could not imagine how anyone could ever have ridden one. The weighty bike pulled him down. He thrashed out for the pedals. Missed them. Found them. With his feet on the pedals and his hands on the handlebars, he felt he had a little control. Again he tried to rear back and level the bicycle out. No, too heavy. Whereas he had been in complete control of the ten-speed, the old bike was in control of him.

At moments he was able to level the bike up and feel as if he were gaining control, but then the bike would dive again as if he were on a giant roller-coaster. The first plunge was the most terrifying, but he was still not at the end of the ride. Each new plunge took his breath away.

As they roared down, his arms aching as he held on, he had the strange sensation that he had only dreamed of the ten-speed. This old bicycle was the one he had always ridden, without comfort, without joy, without control. It was mean, ugly. Why? Why did it seem this was the bicycle he had ridden all his life? Clumsy, inept, uncontrollable.

All these things flashed by as he fought to right the plunge. But each time he tried to work against the old machine, the more purposefully it pulled him down.

At last he realized there was no point trying to fight. For the moment, as they raced downward, he was all right. Disaster waited only at the end of his flight.

He felt he could do nothing to delay the ultimate terror. But he could not prevent himself from fighting back, hopeless as it seemed.

Why? Why was he being forced back? What had happened to his dreams? What of Sam? Had that been a dream, too? When he thought of the dog his anxiety diminished. He remembered the warmth of that furry coat, the soft pant, the presence that seemed to say, "I am always near you. There is nothing you have to do. I'm here."

He was more relieved, relaxed, relaxed enough to look around.

Space still raced by. Whereas before he was able to distinguish objects—stars, galaxies, asteroids, yes, even the moon—now light flashed by him in a blur.

But, coming through the blur, a form not lighted by the other stars, but shining from within itself.

Sam!

The big dog raced toward him. No doubt, Sam! He galloped with the grace of a thoroughbred, ears back, jaws slightly open, tongue to one side, tail straight behind him. Not the popping run of little dogs, but his legs gathering under him as he reached and stretched in a smooth gallop, a symphony of motion, concern, love. Sam!

As fast as Stephan fell, Sam was soon abreast of him. The dog looked neither to the right nor the left. He did not waste his breath barking, but galloped alongside, in concert with Stephan's descent.

With Sam beside him, Stephan bent over the handlebars and began to pedal. He began to get the feel of it. No longer did it seem to control him. As long as he pedaled with it, just as he would any bicycle, it obeyed. Not completely. They still raced down at a frantic speed and, despite the few tentative moves Stephan had made to pull it up, it slanted down even more. But now, Stephan did not panic. He did not fight. Although the bike dove more steeply, he crouched over the handlebars and stayed with it. As he merged with the identity of the bike, it began to surrender itself to him. Yes, he could almost sense it slowing down, and he noticed Sam eased his gallop into a lope.

As they descended he knew that soon he would have to make a decision. He was becoming aware of a large, dark shape looming up. A few of the stars and planets disappeared, cut off by the edge of a more solid horizon. Earth.

As he fell, Stephan recognized the entire sphere, continents, oceans, mountains, finally, cities. He realized he plunged toward the lights of New York.

He must concentrate. Earth rose faster and faster and his path led him toward a darkened patch. The harbor? Central Park? He moved too rapidly to tell.

The ground raced up. He knew he had but one chance. As the ground raced up to meet him, it seemed ringed with brightness. No time to decide if they were stars or lights. He had to act.

He opened and closed his hands alternately. Took a tighter grip. The air whipped by him. He blinked hard to clear his eyes and said to himself, "Now!"

Instead of pedaling forward, he pedaled furiously in reverse. He leaned back as hard as he could. The entire bicycle vibrated with the strain. The rear wheel went down. The front wheel came up, the bicycle leveled out. Stephan hung suspended, no motion at all.

That second seemed to spread out into an eternity. Miracle of miracles, he was no longer on the old bicycle, but on the ten-speed, leisurely back-pedaling for balance as he had done so often in traffic.

In his descent, his arms ached with wrenching pain, his chest felt as if it would burst, and his eyes teared. But now he was strangely at ease. The pain gone, he felt relaxed and comfortable, as he always had when he rode the ten-speed.

He hovered just a few yards above the transverse at Seventy-Second Street in Central Park. He looked about. There was Sam, running circles just as he had when he was a puppy making his first entrance in the park, so happy he did not know where to run first.

"We made it, Sam," Stephan said quietly. "We're safe."

Stephan's relief was immense, but he was also aware that something had come to an end. Sam sensed it, too, and he looked at Stephan as if he expected Stephan to know what to do next.

Stephan knew. The knowing came, as insights usually do, without warning.

92

Where just a few moments before he had plunged downward with such terror, now he and Sam hung motionless, in limbo. Stephan knew what his choices were: to continue to wander in endless space, or to return to his own world.

He wheeled the bike in small, tentative circles. Sam watched. He padded around the bike every now and then, sniffing the wind, looking to Stephan.

It was not unlike those last winter days at the farm when he had come to Stephan and laid his beautiful head in Stephan's head, asking for help. Stephan had known then what he must do, but was afraid. Now he was no longer afraid; sad, but not afraid. There comes a time when all things end, end to make room for more beginnings. In sending Sam through the vet's door that terrible day, he had given something to Sam. Not death, but dignity. And, in accepting, Sam had given back, opened Stephan up.

"I had it all the time," Stephan realized now.

"Sam," he called, and the big dog drew abreast. Stephan reached down and stroked the great head, pulled gently on the silken ears, resolved always to remember how the warmth felt under his hand, knew he would.

"Go on, Sam," he said.

If only he and Dorothy had been able to touch. That's all it takes, to touch. And they had had it all the time, too.

"Go on, Sam, shine. You are the brightest of us all." Then Stephan shifted to high gear and pushed down on the pedals, hard.

Sam leaned his big body against Stephan's leg for the last time and then, with a magnificent leap, bounded off into space.

The bicycle dropped to the ground with no more of a shock than when Stephan got out of bed and put his bare feet on the cold floor of his country home.

Home. Stephan was home.

Epilogue

Stephan stood on the roadway and looked at the sky long after Sam had disappeared. Soon it would be light. Stephan felt it coming more by the trembling which precedes it than by any knowing. And so, too, the dark, as well as Sam, would be gone. No, only the dark. Sam was with him forever. But, for the moment, Stephan could not tell his tears from the stars.

Suddenly he was startled by the squeal of tires and turned just in time to see a yellow taxi brake to a stop just behind him. Instinctively Stephan dodged, pulling the bike with him. Yet it all happened as if in slow motion, curiously without tension.

The driver leaned his head out of the window and said, rather quietly, "You want to get killed?" He had a patrician face with silver-gray hair.

"You saw me," Stephan said. "You actually saw me!"

"Of course, I saw you. Did you think you were invisible?"

"No. I know I'm not invisible." He felt at peace.

"Say, that's a great-looking bike," the driver said. "Is it new?"

Although his face was lined, he had a look of excitement and youth as he stared at the bike.

"No, it's not new."

"Well, you must keep it in good shape, then. But why are you riding so early? It's not that safe, you know."

"I know."

"Do you always ride at this time?"

"No."

"Then what are you doing here now?"

"I just came back from the moon."

The driver looked at Stephan, smiled.

"The moon?" he said. "Then you've seen it all."

"No," Stephan answered, "only the beginning."

The driver laughed.

"Great!" he said. "Come on, I'll follow you out of the park."

Stephen nodded back, then pedaled ahead. They had touched.

Where to? Pia? Dorothy? No, Stephan was no longer alone with that loneliness so desperate it takes the reachers past each other. What would come, would come on its own. Blossom. And soon.

At the entrance to the park, the cabbie waved goodbye and Stephan waved back. Each went his own way.

Lights began to come on in the big apartments, dappling the dawn. The color was subtracted from the city like the understatement in a Chinese painting, but Stephan felt as if all the colors were within himself. As he rode along, he looked up to the great reaches of sky.

He was sure he heard the soft thud of paws as they padded some celestial route away from the flat plane of Earth into the turning parabola of heaven and bright stars.